Come Home to 〈 P9-DDS-978
Five Generations of Pioneer Girls

Martha Morse, Laura's great-grandmother
born 1782
Martha was born to a wealthy landowning family in Scotland. She loved her family, but she also wanted to see the world, and one day she left her home to start a new life in America.

Charlotte Tucker, Laura's grandmother
born 1809
Martha's daughter Charlotte was born a city girl and grew up near the bustling port of Boston. Charlotte had a restless spirit and traveled farther and farther west before settling in Wisconsin.

Caroline Quiner, Laura's mother
born 1839
Charlotte's daughter Caroline spent her childhood in Wisconsin, and her days were busy helping her mother keep their little frontier farm running. Caroline grew up to be Ma Ingalls, Laura's mother.

Laura Ingalls
born 1867
Caroline's daughter Laura traveled by covered wagon across the frontier. When Laura grew up, she realized the ways of the pioneer were ending and wrote down the stories of her childhood in the Little House books.

Rose Wilder, Laura's daughter
born 1886
Laura's daughter, Rose, traveled from South Dakota to the Ozark Mountains of Missouri. She grew up hearing the stories of her mother's frontier girlhood and determined that one day she would be a new kind of pioneer.

The Little House

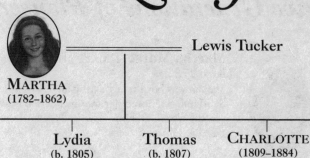

MARTHA
(1782–1862) ——————— Lewis Tucker

Lewis
(b. 1802)

Lydia
(b. 1805)

Thomas
(b. 1807)

CHARLOTTE
(1809–1884)

Joseph
(1834–1862)

Henry
(1835–1882)

Martha
(1837–1927)

Mary
(1865–1928)

LAURA
(1867–1957)

Family Tree ❧

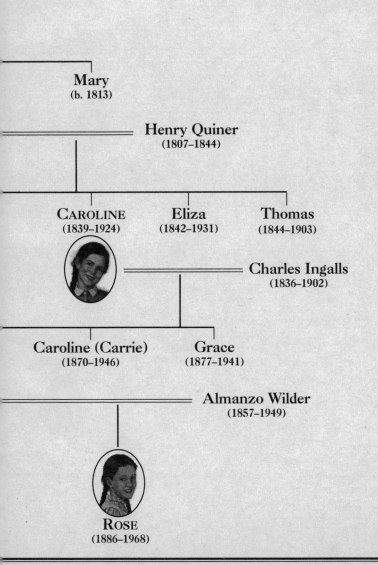

Mary
(b. 1813)

Henry Quiner
(1807–1844)

Caroline
(1839–1924)

Eliza
(1842–1931)

Thomas
(1844–1903)

Charles Ingalls
(1836–1902)

Caroline (Carrie)
(1870–1946)

Grace
(1877–1941)

Almanzo Wilder
(1857–1949)

Rose
(1886–1968)

Little House
by
Boston Bay

Melissa Wiley

Illustrations by Dan Andreasen

HarperTrophy®
A Division of HarperCollinsPublishers

For Kate and Erin

*Special thanks to Amy Edgar Sklansky for her invaluable
help in researching the history and customs of nineteenth-century
Roxbury, Massachusetts. The author also wishes to acknowledge
the contributions of Chris Messier and the costumed interpreters
at Old Sturbridge Village, and of Jack Larkin, Director of
Research, Collections, and Library at Old Sturbridge Village
and author of* The Reshaping of Everyday Life.

Harper Trophy®, 🐾®, Little House®, and The Charlotte Years™
are trademarks of HarperCollins Publishers Inc.

Little House by Boston Bay
Text copyright © 1999 by HarperCollins Publishers Inc.
Illustrations copyright © 1999 by Dan Andreasen

Library of Congress Cataloging-in-Publication Data
Wiley, Melissa.
    Little house by Boston Bay / Melissa Wiley ; illustrations by Dan
Andreasen.
        p.   cm. — (Little House)
    Summary: Living with her family near Boston, five-year-old Charlotte
Tucker, who would grow up to become the grandmother of Laura Ingalls
Wilder, feels the effects of the War of 1812.
    ISBN 0-06-027011-X. — ISBN 0-06-028201-0 (lib. bdg.)
    ISBN 0-06-440737-3 (pbk.)
    [1. Family life—Boston (Mass.)—Fiction.   2. United States—
History—War of 1812—Fiction.   3. Boston (Mass.)—Fiction.]
I. Andreasen, Dan, ill.   II. Title.   III. Series.
PZ7.W64814Lh   1999   99-11748
[Fic]—dc21   CIP
                                                                  AC

6   7   8   9   10
❖
First Harper Trophy Edition, 1999

Contents

The Saturday Family

Mama looked out the kitchen window and said, "Time to get these beans on the plate, Charlotte." Charlotte knew that meant it was Saturday night, and Papa and the boys were walking across the road from the smithy. Papa would stop in the lean-to to wash his hands and face, and then Lewis and Tom would take their turns. By the time they had all scrubbed off the soot of the shop, Mama would have loaded each plate with a steaming heap of baked beans. Baked beans were part of the special supper

1

that belonged to Saturday night.

Ever since Charlotte had turned four, nearly a whole year ago, it had been her job to take the pewter plates off the cupboard shelves and carry each one to Mama at the kitchen hearth. Lydia, nine years old, had the more important task of carrying the full plates to the table in the parlor. Charlotte didn't mind. She liked to climb up on a chair to reach the row of plates lined up on their ends, reflecting back a funny, blurred girl with green eyes big as saucers and a chin even pointier than Charlotte's real one. She liked to climb back down and open the cupboard doors to see all the things inside—the neatly stacked bowls, the candlestick holders, the big round tin that was always full of sugar cookies. It felt comfortable to know what was inside the tin without looking.

Saturday night had that same cozy, comfortable feeling. A Saturday supper was special, for it was a hot meal. Most evenings supper was simply a cold tea of bread and cheese and leftovers, for the big meal of the day was dinner, at noon. Mama seldom cooked at night—except on Saturdays.

Saturday night meant thick pools of corn-meal pudding on the plates beside the baked beans. It meant coffee for Mama and Papa instead of cider. And it meant three things in the middle of the dinner table—the three members of what Charlotte secretly thought of as "the Saturday family." There was the mother, a tall, delicately curved cruet of cider vinegar; the father, a squat redware molasses jug with a jaunty handle and a friendly chip on the rim; and between them, cradled in a china dish, the butter baby.

Charlotte had never told anyone about the Saturday family—it was nice to have a secret all her own. Besides, her brothers would tease her about it. Twelve-year-old Lewis would tease because he was a teasing kind of person, and Tom, who was seven, would tease because he did everything Lewis did. Lydia never teased, but she would be either not at all interested in the secret or much *too* interested, and she would take over the game and change it. Charlotte did not want it to be changed. Like Saturday night itself, the Saturday family was perfect just as it was.

Papa came inside, smelling of coal smoke and horses. His face was red from the scrubbing and from the heat of the forge in his shop. He went to the hearth and kissed the back of Mama's neck below her white linen cap. Mama turned and smiled her special Papa-smile that made her eyes crinkle into crescent moons.

From the lean-to came the splashing, jostling sound of the boys washing up. Papa tugged Lydia's thick red braids to say hello, and he stretched out one of Charlotte's dark ringlets like a spring. Then he bent down to baby Mary, who was playing with a rolling pin on the floor at Mama's feet, and swept her up into his arms.

Mary crowed with delight and tugged enthusiastically on Papa's side-whiskers. Gently he freed her chubby hand and carried her to the lean-to to tell the boys to hurry up.

"Take the sugar bowl, Lydia," Mama said,

"and Charlotte, you put the bread on the table, there's a lass." Carrying the breadboard, Charlotte followed Lydia along the narrow hallway, past the stairs and the front door, into the parlor, where another fire crackled and the late-afternoon sun slanted between the blue curtains.

Soon Mama came into the parlor, tucking wisps of her red hair back into place beneath her cap, and just behind her was Papa, with Mary still in his arms. Mama set Mary into her special high chair and was just scooting it up to the table as Lewis clattered in. Tom came behind him, stout and sturdy as an ox, as Mama always said.

Lewis's red hair was wet around his ears, and his hands dripped from the hurried washing he'd given them in the lean-to. Mama sent him to dry off before Papa said grace. Tom sighed impatiently, eyeing the beans before him.

Everything was just as it always was. Charlotte listened to the fire pop and sigh beneath the sound of Papa's quiet voice as he spoke the words of the blessing. She heard Mary clinking a spoon on the table and Mama softly hushing her. Then Papa said, "Amen," and that was when Charlotte opened her eyes and realized at once that something was not right.

The Saturday father was missing. The vinegar mother (who could be a little bit sour but had a nice tang to her) was there in her usual place, and the fat, dimpled lump of butter was beside her in its little china crib. But the jolly redware jug wasn't there.

Before Charlotte could say anything, Lewis noticed it too. "Lydia forgot the molasses for our pudding!" he announced.

"I did not either forget!" Lydia protested. "There isn't any. Right, Mama?"

"Aye," Mama said. "You ought to be careful about letting your tongue set sail without a compass, Lewis." She winked at him and everyone laughed, because that was just what Mama always said about herself.

"But what happened to the Sat— to the molasses?" Charlotte asked. She had almost said "the Saturday father" but caught herself just in time.

"There isna any," Mama said. "I fear we'll have no more until the blockade is lifted; not even Bacon's store can get it right now. I'm sorry, Lew," she said to Papa. "We'll have to eat our pudding without it."

Cornmeal pudding with molasses was Papa's very favorite of all the new foods he had learned to eat since he had come to America fifteen years ago. He had never eaten molasses in Scotland, where he and Mama had grown up.

But Papa shrugged, smiling his quiet smile. "We canna expect to go withoot makin' some sacrifices noo and then, when there's a war on," he said.

War meant fighting, Charlotte knew, but what did that have to do with molasses?

"What's a blockade?" Tom asked.

Lewis spoke up quickly. "It's when someone blocks a harbor so no ships can get in or out. Those blasted British have got Boston Harbor closed so tight, you couldn't get a rowboat through, let alone a merchant ship."

"Lewis!" Mama said sternly, and Papa raised his eyebrows.

"Beg pardon," Lewis mumbled. "But I'd like to know what I *should* call 'em. They're our enemies, after all."

"Still, that be no excuse for rough language," Papa said.

And Mama demanded, "Have you ivver heard your father usin' such a word?"

A funny look came over Lewis's face. "No, not *Papa* . . ." he said, letting the sentence trail off.

Mama stared at him a moment and then burst out laughing. "Meanin' you've heard *me* use it, I suppose. Och, my mother always said a day would come when my quick tongue would get me into trouble. And here it is, my own son tellin' me I'm a bad influence." She smiled a rueful smile. "All right then, young man, I'll guard me own tongue and you'll guard yours. We ought both of us to follow your father's example and keep our mouths closed more often."

"But then how would you get any work done?" Charlotte asked. Everyone laughed again, and she looked at them in puzzlement. She had not meant to be funny. Mama said the secret to getting work done was knowing the right song to go with it. She had a different song for every task. Even if she was hemming a dress and had her mouth full of pins, she hummed in time to the pinning. Mama said she had gotten the habit as a little girl in Scotland.

Papa and Mama and Lewis went back to talking about the war. Charlotte had been listening to war talk almost her whole life, for the war with England had begun way back in 1812, when she was only three years old. She knew it had something to do with sea battles, and a place called Canada way to the north, and that Mama thought it was a foolish thing and spoke of it scornfully as "Mr. Madison's War." But until tonight it had never seemed to have anything to do with her own life, and Charlotte had not paid much attention to all the talk. Now this mysterious war had taken all the molasses from Boston Harbor. *It* was the reason the poor father jug had to sit empty in the pantry tonight. Whoever Mr. Madison was, Charlotte did not think she liked him—not if his war kept away all the molasses and made people fight.

It was a new idea, and an unsettling one, to think that someone who lived far away and did not even know her could change things right on her own dinner table. No molasses! Charlotte hadn't known molasses came from ships—she'd thought it came from the general store, or the stores in Boston. The comfortable Saturday-night feeling was gone, and the world seemed very big outside the weathered brown door of the Tucker house.

Charlotte looked around the table. No one else seemed to mind. Lewis and Tom thought the war was exciting. Lydia didn't care one way or the other; Mama always said Lydia lived in a world of her own. And Mary was not yet a year old. She didn't even know what molasses was, much less a war.

At least the war had not changed everything about Saturday night. After supper things went on just as they always did: Mama washed the dishes, Lydia wiped them, Charlotte swept beneath the table. Then she put the Saturday mother back on the pantry shelf beside the Saturday father. (The butter baby lived down in the root cellar, where it was nice and cool.) Charlotte felt better when the vinegar cruet and the molasses jug were lined up side by side, even if the jug was empty. And then it was time to help Mama put the salt cod to soak for tomorrow's dinner, which was one of the very best parts of Saturday night. The war began to feel far away again.

Mama took the lid off the codfish barrel, and Charlotte lifted out five of the stiff, dried fish. She laid each one into the big pan of water Lydia had filled. The fish would soak all night, and by tomorrow morning they would be soft enough to cook. Salt cod was Sunday's special dinner, just as baked beans and corn pudding belonged to Saturday night.

Soon it was bedtime. Mama sent Charlotte and Lydia upstairs to their bedchamber to put on their nightclothes. Lydia went carefully ahead of Charlotte, holding a tallow candle in a pewter candlestick. The flame made a yellow circle in the dark. Lydia set the candle on the table by Mama's loom and opened the big wooden press, where the nightgowns were hung. Mama came in to dress Mary for bed. The baby slept with Mama and Papa in the parlor, but her clothes were kept upstairs with Charlotte's and Lydia's.

Charlotte went to the back window and stared out at the blue dark. She could see little bits of darkness waving and quivering in the yard, and she knew it was leaves shaking in the wind. If she stared very hard, she could see the dark shapes of the barn and the privy. The rail fence around the sheep pen made black slashes against the night.

Behind her, Mama was singing a funny song about a corbie and a crow as she wrestled Mary into her nightdress. Charlotte didn't know what a corbie was. She would ask Mama later.

Right now her mind was still turning over the strange new thoughts that had crept into it at supper.

Things were happening in the world, far away. Until now she had not thought of the world as something that spread far beyond Boston. There was her own house on Tide Mill Lane. There was Papa's blacksmith shop across the way, and Washington Street that ran it front of it. There were the other things on that street: the gristmill, the potter's shop, other houses, and down the road the meeting-house and Roxbury Common. If you kept following the road, Charlotte knew, you would get to the city of Boston. Boston seemed to be a kind of grown-up Roxbury, with even more houses and shops and mills. If you needed something that couldn't be found in Roxbury, you went to Boston to get it.

But now it seemed that there were things that came to Boston from *other* places. They came on ships that sailed from other harbors. Molasses was one of those things. Charlotte wondered where molasses started out. That was another thing she must ask Mama.

A clattering noise came from behind her. "Och, Mary!" Mama cried out. "You wee minx, how do you move so fast?"

"I'll get it, Mama," Lydia said.

Mary had knocked a shuttle off the loom; it happened so often, Charlotte could tell without looking. She knew all the house's sounds. That scraping noise, there—that was a chair being pulled across the floor downstairs. Papa liked to sit near the parlor fire and listen to it crackle in its dry, whispery voice. The bumps and thumps next door were the comforting sounds of Lewis and Tom getting ready for the night. Everyone was where he should be. Turning her back on the dark outside, Charlotte went to help Lydia fish Mama's shuttle out from under the loom.

The Corbie and the Crow

Sunday was a quiet day, a day of fish cakes and flapjacks, of best bonnets and go-to-meeting dresses. In his black woolen tailcoat, striped vest, and silver-buckled shoes, Papa looked stern and solemn, not a bit like his weekday self. His long brown hair was tied in back with a black ribbon, and his strong chin was swallowed by a folded neckerchief. Mama had to scold him not to fuss with that neckerchief as often as she scolded Tom and Lewis in their stiff Sunday shirts.

Charlotte and Lydia liked their Sunday

dresses, for they were made of boughten cotton cloth, instead of the plain homespun linen Mama wove for everyday clothes. Lydia's red braids glowed above her rich brown print, and Papa said Charlotte was pretty as a posy in her lilac-colored frock.

Mary was too young to sit still in church, but even so, she wore a special dress on Sundays, as snowy white as the bit of lace at Mama's throat. Mama wore her good Sunday gown, too, even though she could not go to meeting. She was so beautiful in her fine black linen that Charlotte almost wished *she* were old enough to stay home and take care of the baby, so that Mama could go to meeting where all the town could see her.

But it was only an *almost* wish. Charlotte liked going to meeting, though her brothers and sister did not. They minded the long hours of sitting still. Charlotte didn't much like the sitting-still either, but it seemed to her only fair to spend a good long spell of time in the pew—for the pew would be lonely without them the rest of the week. It was Papa's pew; he had paid for it, and no one else could sit in it unless he gave leave.

Then there was the singing, which everyone liked, even restless Lewis. And during the sermon there was the fun of looking at all the people in their best clothes, and guessing who among them was really listening and who was only pretending to.

But the best thing about Sunday was when it was over, for that meant tomorrow was Monday, and Will would come back. Will was a tall young man who worked for Papa in the smithy. He was called a striker, because so much of his work was striking the hot iron with his hammer. He boarded with the Tuckers and took nearly all his meals with them.

Will was taller even than Papa, and his shoulders were thin, not broad like Papa's. He had laughing hazel eyes and an appealing way of furrowing his brow when he listened to someone speak. His hair was cut short, in the new fashion. He wore long, loose-fitting trousers called pantaloons instead of the tight, knee-length breeches Papa wore. Pantaloons had not been around very long, and mostly they were worn by young men.

Mama liked to tease Papa that he was not so very old; he ought to switch to pantaloons too.

"Nay, I think not," Papa would say, shaking his head. "Breeches were good enough for me father, an' sure they be good enough for me." Charlotte didn't mind that Papa wouldn't wear pantaloons. They belonged to Will.

Will came from Dorchester, a town south of Roxbury. It was not far, but it was too far for Will to go home to every night. He went home only for Saturday nights and Sundays.

He always returned on Monday just as the sun was coming up. Today was no different. Upstairs, buttoning up their dark-blue home-spun dresses and tying on their gray muslin aprons, Charlotte and Lydia heard the low rumble of his voice and the lilting sound of Mama greeting him. Then footsteps, and Papa's soft voice. Then the *crash crash crash* of Lewis going down the stairs two at a time, and the *thump thump thump* of heavy-footed Tom following him.

Charlotte and Lydia were the last ones to the kitchen in the mornings, for they must do their upstairs work first. They turned back the covers on their bed to let the sheets air out. Charlotte dusted the bedstead, the wooden chest beneath the window, and the little round table that held the washbasin and pitcher. Lydia swept the floor, singing all the while, for Lydia had Mama's way of singing as she worked. Then they went next door to do the same things in the room Lewis and Tom shared with Will. They did not have to air Will's bed today, since he had not slept in it last night.

When at last they arrived in the kitchen, no one was there. There was only a maze of footprints in the sand on the wooden floor. Mama kept the floorboards covered with a layer of sand, to catch grease and spills. Every night she swept that sand into a pretty pattern of curves and swirls.

There was never much left of the pattern

by the time Charlotte and Lydia came downstairs. The swirls had been scattered by Papa's deep boot prints, and Will's, and the heel-and-toe marks of Lewis's bare feet, with Tom's heavy prints practically on top of them. All around, over and under the others, were Mama's neat light prints. They crossed each other many times between the fireplace and the table, and then they headed out the door to the lean-to. There were no tracks from Mary, for she was still asleep in the parlor.

Lydia went to wake and dress Mary, and Charlotte got the broom out of corner. One of her downstairs chores was to keep the sand off the stone flooring that extended out from the hearth. Mama needed that area clear; when she cooked, she put little heaps of hot coals on the stone. She set iron trivets upon the coals, for heating small pots and skillets.

When Mama needed to use a bigger pot, she hung it from the crane inside the fireplace. The crane was an iron arm that could be swung out away from the flames and then swung back into the fireplace. Mama also kept a kettle of water there all day, so that she had hot water whenever she needed it. A tin dipper hung on a nail beside the hearth, next to the poker and the ash shovel Mama used to pull out the hot coals.

Above the hearth was a shelf lined with all sorts of wonderful objects. Charlotte knew what every one of them was for: the prickly tin nutmeg grater, the potato masher, the shiny tin measuring cups lined up like a row of ducks. She liked the spidery black script on the labels of the spice jars. Each word meant a different smell: *curry, cinnamon, cayenne.* Charlotte could not read the names, but she knew the smells by heart. She could never decide which one smelled best.

Beside the fireplace was a brick bake oven. It was a large square hole built into the wall, with bricks making its top and bottom and sides. The hole was closed off by a metal door. When Mama wanted to bake something, she took off the door and built a fire inside, right on the bricks.

Mama was going to bake today. Even if

Monday hadn't always been baking day, Charlotte would have known by the fire blazing hot and orange in the brick oven.

Before Charlotte had finished sweeping, Mama came in carrying a pail full to the brim with milk.

"Ah, there you are, Lottie," said Mama cheerily, crossing to the pantry and pouring the milk into two wide, shallow pans. "As soon as you've done sweepin', I need you to run down to the root cellar and bring me four good big potatoes."

"Yes, Mama," Charlotte said. She finished quickly, while Mama covered the milk pans with linen towels to keep the flies out while the cream was rising. Charlotte emptied the dustpan out the open window. Then she opened the cellar door and peered down the dark stairs.

"Go in from the outside door, love," Mama said. "If you leave it open, you'll not need a candle."

So Charlotte ran through the lean-to and around the house to the outer cellar door. The air was chill and the sky was still pink at the edges. The unpainted clapboard walls of the house looked gray in the morning light. Mama said they ought to have the house painted one of these years—everyone was painting their homes, nowadays—but there was always so much other work to do that no one had time. It was an old house, older even than Mama and Papa, and it was not as smart as the new houses that were appearing all over Roxbury. But it was sturdy and snug, and Mama said it suited them fine.

Charlotte went around to the back of the house. There was Lewis out in the barnyard forking hay into a pile for the cows, Patience and Mollie, and their two knobby-legged calves. In the shady corners of the yard were a few last clumps of snow, and Charlotte shivered. She didn't know how Lewis could stand to walk on the cold, damp ground in his bare feet.

She hurried down the cellar steps to the big wooden potato bin. A pale rectangle of light fell upon the earthen floor from the open door

at the top of the stairs. Charlotte dug down into the sand and counted out potatoes, two, three, four. They felt cool and firm.

Back in the kitchen, Mama quickly peeled the potatoes and put them in a skillet to fry. Lydia came in from the parlor and handed Mary to Charlotte. The baby's long skirt trailed from Charlotte's lap and reached halfway to the floor.

"Don't let her muss her gown," Lydia told Charlotte. "Today she's wearing lavender silk with ribbons of purest gold."

Of course Mary wasn't really wearing silk. Lydia was only pretending. It would be silly to put real silk and ribbons on the baby—it was hard enough just keeping Mary's plain muslin frock clean.

Lydia went out to feed the chickens, while Charlotte held a squirming Mary upon her lap and watched Mama make the bread dough.

First Mama took out the wooden flour box with the yeast sponge inside. The sponge was a mixture of yeast, cornmeal, rye flour, and water. Mama had mixed it last night and poured it into a hollow in the middle of the rye flour in the flour box.

Last night the sponge had been thin as pancake batter, but during the night it had soaked into the flour and thickened. Now, while Charlotte watched, Mama took off the box cover and scooped handfuls of flour from the corners of the box toward the center. She kneaded the flour into the sponge until she had a thick dough. Then she lifted the big lump of dough out of the box and put it on the table to finish kneading.

At last it was ready to rise. Mama put the dough in a bowl, covered it with a cloth, and left it to sit while she finished making breakfast.

"Go and sweep the parlor, Charlotte," Mama said. "Take Mary with you."

Everyone had chores to do before breakfast. Papa and Lewis fed the cows and the calves and the six wrinkly merino sheep who lived in the barn. Tom filled the woodbox, and Will went across to the smithy to haul the day's coal up from the coal cellar below the shop. And Lydia, after feeding the hens, came back inside to set the table for breakfast.

Charlotte's next job was to sweep the parlor, but she didn't like to do it when the baby was there. Mary clung to her legs and grabbed at her apron, or she sat down right in the middle of the dust pile.

But at last the floor was swept and breakfast was ready. The smell of fried potatoes came out of the kitchen ahead of Mama. There were eggs, too, and cold sliced beef and slices of fried cornmeal pudding. Papa and the boys came in, and Will hurried in from the smithy.

No one talked at breakfast. Everyone was too busy eating. Charlotte was so hungry that she ate two slices of pudding. The pudding made her remember, with some sorrow, the empty molasses jug. Neither Mama nor Papa could say when Mr. Bacon's store would have molasses to sell again.

Then breakfast was over, and Papa, Will, and the boys went across the road to the smithy. Lewis helped Papa in the shop. He worked the long-handled bellows that blew air onto the coals in the forge to make them hotter; he swept the floor and fetched tools for Papa and Will.

Tom wasn't tall enough to work the bellows yet. But he helped fetch tools too.

Mama told Lydia to begin clearing the table. To Charlotte she said, "Come, you can help me bring in the water."

Outside they found Will already at the well, filling two big buckets with water for the smithy. In Papa's shop was a great wooden tub that must always be kept filled, for plunging hot iron in to cool it.

Charlotte was always glad to see Will Payson, with his pantaloons and his quick laugh. She liked to talk to him, for he listened just as carefully to small girls of almost five as he did to mothers and fathers. He never laughed when someone asked a question, even if everyone else in the room did.

She liked to listen to him talk, too, for he knew a great many interesting things. Birds, for example—he knew everything there was to know about them. He could tell the name of a bird just by looking at its nest or listening to its song. When he whistled, he sounded so much like a real bird that Charlotte half expected to see one perched on his head.

Once, last month, Charlotte and Tom had come upon Will standing among the trees behind the smithy, watching a small brown bird hop among the old leaves on the ground. The bird had a white chest and red patches on its sides, and Will said she was called a towhee, after her song. He whistled to her, softly, "To-whee! To-whee!" and the bird cocked her head and answered. Her fluty call seemed to say *Drink-your-TEA! Drink-your-TEA!* Tom and Charlotte burst out laughing, for it *was* nearly teatime, and Will often got so absorbed in watching birds that he was late to the table. Their laughter startled the bird and she flew away. But Will said she would come back, for she was nesting; he showed them the small nest half hidden in the brush, with five tiny speckled eggs inside.

Charlotte liked Will so much that for a while she had had a secret plan for Lydia to marry him as soon as she was old enough. That way Will would always stay with the family. Charlotte would have married him herself, but Lydia would be old enough sooner. It seemed best not to wait too long.

But now Will was telling Mama that he was going to marry a girl named Lucy. She lived in Dorchester, not far from his father's farm, Will explained. Just as soon as he had saved enough money for a house, he was going to bring Lucy to Roxbury to live.

"You'll like her, Mrs. Tucker," he told Mama. "She's a lot like you—does her churning on Monday."

Charlotte was confused. "But we churn on Thursdays," she said.

Mama laughed. "That's just Will's way o' sayin' that his Lucy has ideas of her own," she said. "Doesna do what the neighbors do just because it's always been done that way."

"Oh," Charlotte said. Here was something else to think about. The war, ships carrying molasses from someplace far away, Mr. Madison, a corbie—she still had not remembered to ask Mama what that was—and now this idea that it was sometimes good to do things differently from the neighbors. Why *shouldn't* you churn your butter on Thursdays? Everyone she knew did. It seemed to Charlotte that strange new ideas met her at every turn. Just when you thought you understood a thing, something new came along for you to figure out.

Well, it was not hard to understand that she was not going to have Will for a brother after all. At least he wasn't going to move away. He would bring Lucy to Roxbury, and maybe he would build his house nearby. Then Charlotte could visit them. That would be almost as nice as having Lydia marry Will. In fact, in some ways it might be even nicer— there was always the chance this Lucy was the sort of person who believed in giving doughnuts or taffy to little girls who came to visit. Charlotte hoped so.

Will took his buckets of water and turned back toward the smithy.

31

"Och, we must hurry, Charlotte," Mama said. "The oven will soon be ready for baking, and I've not yet made my pies." Quickly they filled the water pails and took them into the house.

By the time Charlotte and Lydia had washed and dried the breakfast dishes and Mama had rolled out two piecrusts, the fire in the brick oven had burned to coals. That meant the oven was hot enough to cook food now—too hot, in fact, for the bricks soaked up so much heat that Mama would have to let the oven cool down a little first, or her pies and bread would burn. She took the wooden ash shovel and scraped the hot embers out of the oven. Beside the oven hung a long-handled brush, and this Mama used to wipe away the last of the ashes. Then she hurried to her piecrusts and quickly put together two dried-apple pies, well sprinkled with cinnamon and brown sugar, with big lumps of butter beneath the strips of pastry on top.

Now it was time to check the oven to see if it had cooled enough to cook the pies.

Mama had a special way to tell when it was cool enough. Charlotte had watched her so many times that she knew how to do it too. She had never done it before, but today she thought she would help Mama. She stuck her arm into the oven and held it there very still.

"Mercy, lass!" Mama cried. But then she saw that Charlotte was being careful not to touch the oven walls.

Charlotte counted, "One, two, three . . ." She got as far as seven before her arm began to feel scorched. She pulled it out and waved it in the cool air. "Still too hot, Mama," she said.

"Aye, I'd say so," Mama said, staring at Charlotte. "Gracious, you gave me a turn."

"Yes, ma'am," Charlotte said. She did not see why Mama should be so suprised. She had only done what Mama did herself to check the oven.

In a few minutes Mama said Charlotte might check it again. This time Charlotte could keep her arm inside all the way to ten.

That meant the oven was just the right temperature for pies. Mama slid the pies into place using the flat, long-handled wooden bread peel. She closed the oven door. While the pies baked, she mixed up a cake to put in the oven after the bread. The brick oven took so much work and used so much wood, Mama did all her week's baking at once.

A sweet, spicy smell soon filled the kitchen. The pies were finished. Mama took them out and put the soft brown lump of bread dough into the oven.

Now the morning rush was over, and the house was calm and quiet. While the bread baked, Mama helped Lydia and Charlotte make the beds: first the upstairs beds, where the sheets were all aired out, and then Mama and Papa's big mahogany bed in the parlor, with its beautiful blue-and-white woven coverlet. The pattern on the coverlet was called "cat tracks and snail trails," for it looked as if a cat with blue paint on its paws had walked across a snowfield, and then a snail had gone through the paint as well and wound in and out among the cat prints.

Charlotte loved that coverlet. She wished she could sleep under it. The cover on her and Lydia's bed was just a quilt made from old red dresses and white linen sheets.

While they worked, Charlotte asked Mama about the corbie.

"It's a kind of bird," Mama explained. "A great black bird like a crow, with a raspin' kind of cry like the sound o' Papa's file against a bit o' metal."

"Oh!" Charlotte said. She thought about it for a minute. "I'm going to ask Will to show me one."

But Mama said she had never seen a corbie in America. They were Scottish birds.

As she smoothed the coverlet over her pillow and Papa's, Mama sang the song for Charlotte and Lydia.

> *"The corbie wi' his roupy throat*
> *Cried frae his leafless tree,*
> *'Come o'er the loch, come o'er the loch,*
> *Come o'er the loch wi' me.'*

"The crow put up his sooty head
And cried, 'Where to? Where to?'
'To yonder field,' the corbie said,
'Where there is corn enoo.

"'The plowman plowed the land yestreen,
The farmer sowed this morn;
And we can make a full, fat meal
Frae off the broadcast corn,
And we can make a full, fat meal
Frae off the broadcast corn.'"

Charlotte listened hard, so the words would stick in her head. She wanted to sing it to Will. He had never been to Scotland, so he did not know about corbies.

Spring

That was the week spring came to stay. April faded into May in a green haze that crept over fields and treetops. The little purple crocuses that had peeped up through the snow were all gone now, and so was the snow. Robins hopped about in the brown garden and sunned themselves on the garden wall. Fragrant buds swelled and burst into bloom on the lilac bush beside the kitchen door.

The speckled eggs hatched in the towhee's

nest. Will took Charlotte to see the five wide-mouthed nestlings peeping shrilly to their mother and her black-feathered husband. Charlotte could have stayed all day watching them, but Will said they would get on better if they were left to themselves. Whenever Charlotte went out, she listened for the mother's gentle voice, reminding the world to *drink-your-TEA, drink-your-TEA.*

Every morning now Lewis turned the six merino ewes out to graze in the meadow behind the garden. Their gray wool was long and curly, and soon it would be time for Papa to shear them. Then Mama would be busy for weeks, washing the fleeces and combing them smooth.

The calves were not so knobby legged anymore. They ran about the barnyard, sturdy and playful. One afternoon Mr. John Heath came and took them away. He tied a rope around each of their necks and led them out of the barn and across the road toward his fields.

Charlotte watched them go. They shook

their shaggy heads from side to side at the strange feeling of the rope. Without them the barn felt lonely. Patience and Mollie stood looking through the wooden slats of their stalls, lowing mournfully.

Charlotte felt sorry for the cows. She wished just once Papa would keep their calves. But every year he traded them for a side of beef and the use of Mr. Heath's plow and oxen. Papa said it was not worth keeping oxen himself, just for plowing the kitchen garden and a few fields of hay and corn. Mr. Heath sent his son Hobson to do the plowing, for Papa could not spare a day from the smithy.

Spring was Papa's busiest season. Farmers from miles around came to his shop for repairs and tools, and pots and pans, and door hinges and horseshoes and wagon parts. They brought the long-toothed harrows they used for breaking up the stony ground before plowing. They brought plowshares and ox chains and harnesses with iron buckles. Anything with iron parts that needed fixing, Papa could fix.

And if it couldn't be fixed, he could make a new one.

Sometimes Mama looked out the kitchen window at the smithy and shook her head. She said it was a wonder Papa ever got any work done at all, with the crowd of men and boys that was always hanging about over there. The farmers who brought in their tools, or their horses to be shod, liked to stay and talk for a while, exchanging news.

When Papa and Will and Lewis came home for tea, Mama scolded them about it. "You ought to send those fellows home to their farms," she said.

But Papa only smiled and said he liked to listen to the chatter while he worked.

"All the same," Mama teased, "they're no more than a bunch of gossips. If there's aught worse than gossipy hens, 'tis gossipy roosters."

This made Lewis sputter indignantly, his face turning red between his freckles. It wasn't gossip, he said—it was important talk about the war. Lewis was very interested in the war news, and he had taken to reading the

40

newspapers whenever he could get one. In the evenings after tea, he spread the papers on the parlor table and shouted about the battles being fought far away on land and sea.

In May there was news of a British fleet headed toward the American troops at Niagara. The account in the paper made Lewis jump up and down until Mama scolded him to behave like a boy and not a bullock with a bee sting.

"But Mama!" Lewis cried. "It says the British were expected to arrive by the fourth or fifth of May. That's yesterday! Our boys could be whupping them right this minute and we wouldn't know it, it takes so long for news to get through."

He pounded the table with his hand, making Lydia jump. She had spread the contents of Mama's thread basket on the table in front of her and was sorting colors for her embroidery sampler.

"Lewis!" she complained.

"Easy, lad," Papa said from the corner where he sat playing at checkers with Will.

"Yes, Papa," Lewis said, abashed. He sat back down at the table with the inky sheets spread out before him. Beside him Tom leaned forward on his elbows to look at the drawings of ships and battle sites.

The evenings were growing longer now, and though the mantel clock had chimed half past six, there was still a golden light coming in the windows. It spilled over the walls and made the pale-blue stripes on the wallpaper shine like silver.

The parlor was the prettiest room in the house. On one side, between the two front windows, was the dinner table where Lewis and Lydia sat. There were eight chairs around the table and yet more chairs lined up along the north wall, next to Mama and Papa's bed. In the middle of the room was a large hooked rug that Mama had made from bits of dyed wool; it had a design of a cheerful, bright-windowed house flanked by apple trees. On the mantel, next to the gleaming wooden clock, was a painted tin platter with yellow and red flowers on a field of black. Charlotte thought it was a grand room, and she felt very proud when company came.

Mama sat in the big upholstered chair by the west window, where she could work without lighting a candle until the sun went down altogether. But the east side of the room was too dim for reading, and so Mama let Lewis have a tallow candle on the dinner table. The burning candle filled the room with a smoky smell and made shadows dance upon the ceiling.

Charlotte sat on the floor at Mama's feet playing a game with a thimble and a button. The thimble was a house, the button a little man who lived there alone. Mary wanted to play too, only she seemed to think both button and thimble looked like nice things to eat.

"Give it back, Mary," Charlotte said, trying for the hundredth time to pry open her sister's chubby fist.

Will scooped Mary up and rescued Charlotte's button. "Here you are, Lottie," he said. "I'll mind the baby for a while."

Charlotte smiled at him gratefully. Will sat back down in his corner chair and gave Mary some of the wooden checkers he had captured from Papa.

"Go on, Lewis," Mama said. "What else does the paper have to say?"

Mama said half of what was written about the war was pure nonsense, but she made Lewis read the papers aloud nonetheless. She sat bolt upright in her chair, knitting furiously and looking as if she might fly up into the air if the news was against her liking.

Will liked to tease Mama by bringing home *The Yankee*. That was a newspaper that supported Mr. Madison and the war, and it outraged Mama. Charlotte had found out that Mr. Madison was the President. She knew about presidents because of General George Washington. He had been the very first President of the United States, and every February there was a big celebration to honor his birthday.

Mr. Madison was the fourth President. There was no parade on his birthday. Will said perhaps there would be someday, when people came to see that he had done the right thing by declaring war on England.

"Surely you don't hold with the British navy boarding American ships and kidnapping our own sailors, Mrs. Tucker," he asked Mama. "Nor riling up the Indians against us and supplying them with arms."

"Of course not," Mama replied tartly. "But you know as well as I do that that business is only part of the story. Our government wants Canada, plain and simple. As if the President hasn't enough on his hands already, tryin' to keep America in one piece."

"Well, noo, we must be fair, Martha," Papa said. "Mr. Madison was no more eager to declare war on England than we are to be in it. Pushed into it, he was, by those land-hungry war hawks from the western territories."

"If I was President, I wouldna let meself be pushed into anything," said Mama.

Papa and Will exchanged a look. "I've nae doubt aboot that," Papa murmured.

"At any rate," said Will, "we're in it now,

and we'd better win. I don't fancy the notion of having this country fall back under England's rule. My father nearly lost his life in the War for Independence. I'm an American, by gum, and I plan to remain one."

"I too," said Papa, in his quiet way.

Charlotte took the button man out of his house and walked him along a long narrow road made by the edge of a floorboard. He came to a table leg and with great exertion climbed up it to peep over Lewis's arm at a tall-masted ship sailing on a flat white newspaper sea.

"Is that the molasses ship?" Charlotte asked. "The one that can't get through because of the clockade?"

Lewis guffawed. "It's *block*ade, you ninny," he crowed.

Tom laughed, and worse, so did Lydia. It was infuriating; Lydia paid so little attention to the war that Charlotte doubted she even remembered why the molasses was gone.

"Easy, now," Mama chided. "I'll not have

you mockin' each other."

"Beg pardon, Mama," Lewis said. "It's just so funny!"

Charlotte started to retort, but Will spoke up first. "As I recall, the ship in that drawing is a sloop-of-war, isn't she, Lewis? Your molasses ship would be a merchant vessel, Charlotte, from New Orleans or the West Indies."

"See, Lottie," said Lewis, not wanting to be left out, "here are the cannons. That's how you can tell she's a warship. This one is British. They've got her anchored off the coast of Connecticut, ready to attack one of our forts."

Charlotte thought a sloop-of-war sounded interesting. It was a good, sensible name, for it told you exactly what sort of a ship it was. But the ship could not be a nice one, if it was going to attack an American fort.

Attacks and blockades, ships and armies— lately the grown-ups and Lewis never seemed to talk about anything but the war. The more

Charlotte heard, the more she worried. What would happen if America lost the war? Suppose it meant there would never be any molasses again—ever? Perhaps there would be a lot of other changes, too.

"There, that's finished," Mama said. She stood and held her knitting up to the window. It was a gray stocking for Papa. Its mate was already finished, and Mama took that one out of her workbasket and folded the two stockings together. A year ago those stockings had been crinkly wool on the back of one of those merinos. Papa had sheared the fleece from the sheep's back, and Mama had washed it and combed it smooth with her spiky-toothed carding brushes. Then she had spun it into yarn on her spinning wheel. And now that yarn had been knitted into a pair of stockings.

Charlotte looked at these stockings, flat and soft and gray in Mama's hands. It seemed to her they were made of more than just wool. There were words and thoughts knitted into them like the tiny prickles of grass seed that sometimes stayed stuck in the wool even after it had been washed and carded and spun. All the words that had been spoken while Mama's quick hands made the needles cross and uncross around the endless strand of wool—all those words about the war, and Mr. Madison, and the cannon-heavy ships—they were all there, knitted into Papa's stockings.

The clock ticked on the mantel, and the newspaper rattled in Lewis's hands. Mama laid the stockings on the table beside her. She stuck her knitting needles through the ball of leftover yarn and dropped the ball into her workbasket.

Charlotte climbed up into Mama's lap. Mama stroked her hair and cuddled Charlotte against her. Charlotte held the thimble tightly in her hand with the button man tucked inside it. The thimble was the button man's bed now, and it was time to go to sleep.

In the Garden

Planting time was passing. The beans and the peas were tucked into their rows. The squashes were planted, and the melons and radishes and turnips. Mama kept Lewis home from the smithy one day to get the potatoes into the ground. And every few days Mama checked *The Farmer's Almanack* to make sure the garden was coming along on schedule.

She sat in her armchair and turned the pages between their yellow covers. There was a pair of pages for each month of the year.

The almanac told when to plant certain crops and when to harvest them. It said what the weather would be like, and when the moon would be full. It told when elections were to be held, and how to save your apple trees from caterpillars, and lots more things besides. There was a list of all the ships in the navy, which Lewis had read so many times that the almanac fell open to that page by itself.

Charlotte wished she could read it, too, but she could not read yet. When school started in June, then she would learn. She already knew a few letters. Mama told her that the letters M-A-Y at the top of the page spelled the word "May," and that was what month it was. On the left-hand page, Mama said, were the words "MAY hath 31 Days." The right side said "MAY, fifth Month," and below that was a verse. Lydia especially liked that verse, and she asked Mama to read it so often that soon even Charlotte began to know it by heart.

It went:

The little wood songsters are tunefully
*   singing,*
To hail the glad morning of each rising day;
And with their shrill echo, the vallies are
*   ringing—*
How sweet are their notes that descend from
*   each spray.*

Charlotte's birthday was in the next-to-last week of May. The almanac said to expect rain in plenty all that week, and it was right. It kept right on raining on the morning of her birthday. Mama said that was a lucky thing, for if it had been fine, they'd have had to work all day in the garden. Instead, after dinner, Mama put Mary in bed for a nap and called Lydia and Charlotte into the cozy corner beside the kitchen hearth. She said Charlotte was five now, and that was old enough to sew doll clothes.

"But I don't have a doll," Charlotte said. Her heart thumped a little because it was her birthday.

"Aye, I suppose that's so—for the moment,"

Mama said, glancing at Lydia. Lydia giggled, her eyes shining with a secret she wanted to tell.

Mama reached into her apron pocket and brought out a clothespin. Charlotte felt a rush of disappointment, but then she saw that Mama had painted a face on the round knob at the top of the clothespin. The doll had round black eyes and a smiling red mouth, and glossy wings of painted black hair parted in the middle. She had little arched eyebrows and red dots for cheeks.

The rest of her was just wooden clothespin. Mama said it was up to Charlotte to dress her, and to think of a name. There were so many names to choose from, Charlotte could not decide. But Mama said naming was a grave matter, and it was wise to think on it awhile.

Lydia was still eager with more of the secret. "What about the dress, Mama?" she asked.

Mama's hand went to her apron pocket again. "I've cut a bit o' cloth for you," she told Charlotte. "'Tis up to you to turn it into a frock."

Mama's hand opened and showed Charlotte a square of fabric. Charlotte squealed in surprise, and Lydia clapped her hands.

"It was my idea," she said.

Mama laughed. "Aye, you've got your sister to thank for this. I'd forgotten I had it tucked away."

The cloth was a piece of a gown Mama had worn long ago. It was a lovely plaid with dark-blue and pale-blue stripes crossing each other. It came from Scotland, where Mama had grown up. She said all the girls in her county had worn blue-plaid gowns and petticoats like this. Now Charlotte's doll could look just the way Mama had as a girl.

Lydia showed Charlotte how to bend a piece of wire around the clothespin for arms while Mama cut a dress pattern out of brown paper. She helped Charlotte trace the pattern onto the pretty cloth, and then she cut it out. Charlotte already knew how to sew a nice straight hem; Mama had made her practice on a sheet all winter long. Charlotte hadn't enjoyed it. But now, Mama said, Charlotte would learn the fun of sewing.

"I hated sewing until I made my first frock for one o' my bairns," Mama explained. "There's naught sweeter than puttin' tiny wee stitches into a gown for your own wee babe. You'll see, now you have a bairn o' your own."

Mama was right. Charlotte liked hemming the doll's dress much better than hemming sheets. She sewed all afternoon and finished the hem before tea. Mama said she would help Charlotte trim the dress and make a petticoat tomorrow, if it rained again.

But the next day was sunny. Mama threw open all the doors in the morning, to air out the house. The little wood songsters made a cheery noise among the apple blossoms in the side yard. The air smelled sweet. Mama said it was a good day to plant. No more rain was expected for a while, according to the almanac.

Mama spread a piece of canvas sacking on the ground beside the garden wall and put Mary on it. The long trailing skirt of Mary's baby frock fanned out next to her, and Mama pinned it down with a stone so that Mary could play on the canvas but couldn't crawl away. "Now stay you there," Mama said. Lydia brought the baby some leaves to play with, but Mama said she might eat them.

"Get the rolling pin, Charlotte," Mama said. "That'll keep her busy awhile."

The vegetables were all planted now, so it was time to plant herbs between the rows. Mama brought out the seeds she had saved from last fall, little specks of black and brown in small brown-paper envelopes sealed with flour paste. Those specks did not look anything like the plants they would become, but Mama knew exactly which speck would turn into which herb, and how deep to plant it.

Mama knew everything there was to know about herbs. All summer she collected them and hung them to dry in upside-down bunches from the lean-to's rafters. Sage and lavender and rosemary, pennyroyal and thyme and hyssop. Bee balm, betony, candytuft—the names were like a song. Mama knew just which ones to add to soup or stuffing to make it tastier, and which ones to flavor cakes with. She could brew them into teas that cured illness or helped you to sleep. She dried them and sewed the crumbly leaves inside little cloth pillows that she sold to Mr. Bacon's store, or traded to the neighbors. Those pillows smelled lovely, and if you put one between your sheets, it kept bedbugs away. It seemed there was nothing you couldn't do with the right combination of herbs, if you just knew how.

Mama poured a packet of lovage seeds into Charlotte's palm. She showed Charlotte how to cup her hand so the wind would not carry the tiny grains away. Taking up her hoe, Mama went along the rows making holes for the seeds. Charlotte tucked one or two seeds into each hole, and Lydia came behind, covering them up with earth.

"What is lovage for?" Charlotte asked. Lydia was singing the little songsters verse to herself. She was putting it to the tune of "Yankee Doodle," only she had to sing the words very quickly to squeeze them all into each melody line. It sounded like:

"Thelittlewoodsongstersaretunefullysinging,
Tohailthegladmorningofeachrisingday."

Mama said lovage leaves tasted delicious in salads and soups. They soothed bee stings, too, she said, and they could be boiled in water to make medicine for the eyes and throat. "Some folks even take the root and candy it in a sugar syrup," she said, "though I've never tried that meself."

"How do you know all that, Mama?"

"I learned it when I was a lass," Mama said, "from a neighbor. An old woman who lived away out on the moor at the edge of me father's land."

"But how did she know?" Charlotte asked.

"I suppose she learned from her mother, or her mother's mother."

"But how did *they* know?" Charlotte persisted. "Who figured it out first?"

"Ah, we'd a story about that when I was

young," Mama said. Lydia stopped singing to listen. "'Twas about a great hero who was killed in a battle. It's said that when he died, herbs sprang up in the grass where his body fell, each one holdin' a fragment of his strength. Beneath his stout heart that never knew fear, there grew a lily-of-the-valley. To this day its root holds the power to stimulate the heart. Where his head lay came a wee green herb that could cure headaches and wounds of the head. Betony, it was. And another, a tall spike of purple flowers with dark spots in their throats, that had been crushed beneath the warrior's middle—people found it made a good strong medicine to make you bring up something that's ailin' your stomach."

"Foxglove!" Charlotte cried. Mama had made a medicine out of foxglove for the miller's wife last winter. It came up by itself every year over by the garden wall. The green stems were getting tall already, and the pale buds would open soon.

"Aye," Mama said, pleased. "Fairy glove,

we called it in Scotland. And that puts me in mind of another tale me mother used to tell."

Charlotte and Lydia begged Mama to tell it. They had come to the end of one row, and now Mama turned and started down another. The hoe made a *chunk, chunk* sound in the soil, and Lydia's hands went *pat, pat*. The seeds did not make any noise falling into their holes. Mama's voice when she began to speak was low and lilting, as if the words were coming from far away.

Mama's Story of the Fairy's Nursemaid

A fine young woman of Aberfeldy there was, who bore her first child in the winter. One evening as she sat by her fire singin' to her bairn, a beautiful lady came into her cottage, dressed in a fairy mantle. The fairy lady carried a bairn, wrapped all in green silk, that cried and fussed in her arms.

"What shall ye do for my child?" asked the lady, her eyes starin' at the young mother

with a fearsome light. The young woman—
Meggie was her name—was that afraid of
the fairy lady, she hardly knew what to say,
but the squallin' of the fairy's bairn went
straight to her heart, and she said, "Give
me the child to nurse."

"Do that, and ye'll nivver want," said
the pretty lady, and with that she gave the
bairn to Meggie. Quick as lightning, she
was gone.

Meggie nursed the fairy's bairn right
alongside her own bonny son. The poor
hungry bairn stopped its terrible wailin',
and when it had taken its fill, it fell fast
asleep wi' a little smile on its wee ugly
face—for as everyone knows, an uglier
thing than a fairy's bairn there isn't in all
the world.

Meggie put the bairn to sleep alongside
her own son that night and tended it as
kindly as if it were her child.

The next morning, to her great surprise, she found two little suits of clothes
laid out on the table, just the sizes to fit

the fairy's bairn and her own bonny son. And a loaf of fine bread there was—fairy bread, that tastes of honey and fills you with more vigor than meat. Meggie took it gratefully and ate some every morning, and on the seventh day it was still as fresh and halesome as it had been the very first morn.

Every week after that a fairy loaf appeared on Meggie's table, and plenty o' fine clothes to keep the two bairns snug all the winter through. The fairy's bairn grew strong and hearty, and soon was as pretty a baby as Meggie's own handsome child. Sure and Meggie did treat the two of them just the same, and a kinder mother there never was.

On a midsummer afternoon the fairy lady came back. Her silken mantle swirled about her face, and her golden hair shone in the sunlight. She looked at her bairn and was pleased to see what a fine, healthy child it had grown into. It clapped its little hands wi' joy to see its mother. The lady took the child into her arms and thanked Meggie for tendin' it so well.

"Follow me now," said the lady, and Meggie picked up her own child and followed. They walked out of the house and through the barley field, and they kept on goin' until they came to a silvery wood on a green hill. At the far edge of the wood, where the sun shone on the slope, a door opened in the green grass of the hillside.

The fairy stooped and plucked a spike of foxglove growing at the foot of one o' the silver trees. She tipped a bloom into her hand and poured out a few drops of a sparkling nectar. Three drops of this dew did she dab onto Meggie's left eyelid. Then Meggie followed the lady through the green door into a land lovelier than anything she had ever seen or imagined. All green and golden and blue, it was, with clear streams and rich fields and trees laden with fruit. At the foot of the tallest tree was a chest filled with webs of fine cloth, and salves and ointments to cure any ill, and more of those honey-sweet loaves Meggie had eaten all the winter through.

"For you," said the fairy lady, "and a mount to carry it home." Up trotted a beautiful snow-white pony led by a little crooked gnome, who lifted the chest onto the pony's back and bid it to follow her home.

Then the lady breathed gently on Meggie's eye, and just like that, all of it was gone—the lady, the fairy bairn, the old gnome, the beautiful green-and-golden country. Meggie found herself back at the edge of the silver wood, her little son held tight in her arms and the white pony nibblin' at the grass with the chest o' treasures on its back.

But Meggie happened to catch sight o' the foxglove spike the fairy had plucked, and she put her finger in the blossoms to see if there was anything left o' the magic dew the fairy had dropped on her eye. Sure enough, there was the tiniest wee bit left, and this did Meggie dab onto her eyelids just as the fairy lady had done.

Then Meggie went home with all the treasures the lady had given her. A long and happy life she had, and always she had the gift of seeing sprites and fairies that were hidden from other mortals. Meggie kept it always a secret that she had this power, until one day many years later she happened to spy the beautiful fairy lady whose child she had nursed. Meggie ran to the lady and took her hand, asking how the fairy child was and sayin' she hoped it had grown up as well and hearty as her own son had.

The fairy gasped and stared at Meggie.

"What eye do ye see me with?" she asked.

"Why, with them both," answered Meggie, and with that the fairy leaned forward and breathed on Meggie's eyes. And from that day forth Meggie could see fairies no more.

* * *

"But she got off lucky," Mama added, "for the fairy lady might have taken away *all* Meggie's eyesight and left her blind. Fairies are touchy things, and it's dangerous to meddle wi' them. It was foolish of Meggie to take that dew, when she'd already been so well rewarded for her kindness."

But Charlotte didn't think so. If she'd been Meggie, she'd have done just the same thing. She wished the foxglove would hurry up and bloom. She would like to try that trick of putting the fairy dew on her eyelids, even if it was a dangerous thing to do.

The Road to Scotland

One day, after planting time had passed and before weeding time had come around, Mama went to Mr. Bacon's store. There she bought a piece of creamy white muslin, which she said was to be a new school apron for Charlotte. Charlotte was surprised to hear it was time to go to school. Last summer's school term seemed so long ago that she had forgotten all about it.

Last summer Charlotte had gone to school with Lydia and Tom. Now Lydia was too old for the summer term. The big boys and girls went only in the winter. Papa needed Lewis in the shop and in the hayfield, and Mama must have Lydia's help around the house and garden. Mostly Lydia watched Mary so Mama could work.

Charlotte was not sure she wanted to go to school. Just now there was so much going on at home, she hated to miss it. She would miss the vegetables getting ripe in the garden and, later on, the picking and the canning and the pickling.

"Who will sweep the hearth while I'm at school, Mama?" she asked.

Mama touched Charlotte's cheek and said, "Lydia will do it. School's naught but three months, Charlotte. You must get every bit of it that you can."

Lydia, who was rocking Mary in the corner, made a face. She would rather go to school to see her friends than stay home and mind the baby.

Mama pushed her needle into Charlotte's school apron and pulled it out. "Lottie, run out to kitchen and tell me if the chicken needs windin' up."

The chicken was roasting on a string in front of the kitchen fire. Mama had tied a string to a nail in the mantelpiece. To the other end of the string she had tied the chicken, which she spun around and around so that the string kinked up in a tight corkscrew. When she let it go, the string untwisted, quickly at first and then slower and slower, turning the chicken around before the flames so that it cooked evenly, all the way through. When the string untwisted all the way, Mama had to wind it up again. A three-legged skillet sat on the hearth below the chicken to catch the drippings. After the chicken had finished roasting, Mama would make a gravy of the drippings with flour, salt, and pepper.

Charlotte saw that there was still plenty of twist left in the string. "It's all right, Mama," she called.

"Good," Mama said. "Run along and play, then."

"Yes, ma'am," Charlotte said.

She wandered out to the garden. The beans were getting tall, their long curling vines climbing up the wooden stakes Mama had pushed into the ground. The newly planted herbs were beginning to sprout. Tiny green spikes peeked out of the soil.

Charlotte had a sudden thought and ran over to the garden wall. Yes, there it was. The foxglove had bloomed at last—spotted purple cups held open to the sun and the wind.

Please work, Charlotte begged silently. She put a finger into a flower cup. It was not wet inside as she had expected it to be. There was only a kind of soft, velvety, sticky feeling. She hoped this was what the fairy dew was supposed to feel like. She knew she must not put foxglove in her mouth, but Mama had never said she couldn't touch it. Holding her breath, she rubbed her finger across both eyelids. Then she opened her eyes, and she waited.

She looked all around. She did not see anything out of the ordinary. No beautiful golden-haired ladies in flowing green mantles, no funny bent gnomes, no ugly, red-faced babies peeping up at her from the comfrey leaves. She walked all around the garden. She climbed the stone wall and stood upon it searching in every direction, and still she saw no fairies.

Just when she was beginning to feel discouraged, she remembered that fairies were like corbies—they lived in Scotland, not America. All of Mama's fairy stories were about Scotland, weren't they?

It took no more than a second for Charlotte to make up her mind. She must go to Scotland. She wanted very badly to see a fairy with her own eyes. Besides, she had already used the fairy dew, and if she did not see a fairy, it would be wasted. Mama said it was a sin to waste anything.

Mama and Papa had come from Scotland to Boston—first Papa, and then, a few months later, Mama had joined him. They had come together from Boston to Roxbury. Charlotte knew just how to get to Boston, and she supposed once she got there, she could ask for directions to Scotland. Mama said Scotland was across the sea, which was evidently a big water like the brook that cut through Roxbury, perhaps a little bigger. There was a bridge across Stony Brook, and Charlotte felt certain there would be a bridge across the sea to Scotland, too.

But the first thing to do was to get to Boston. When Papa went to Boston, he usually borrowed a wagon, to carry things home in. But Mama made the trip on foot sometimes, to do shopping. Even Lydia had been there, once or twice, when Mama needed an extra set of hands for packages.

Lydia said you walked along Washington Street right through the center of town and beyond, until you came to the Neck. The Neck was the part of Washington Street that connected Roxbury to Boston. Lydia had told Charlotte all about how the road there crossed over a shallow bay.

Charlotte was pretty sure that a bay was another kind of water like Stony Brook or the sea. That meant she would cross over three big waters to get to Scotland: first Stony Brook, and then the bay, and then the sea.

It did not sound so hard. Charlotte went into the kitchen to switch her everyday bonnet for her good Sunday one. Mama always wore her best bonnet when she went to Boston.

The roasting chicken was beginning to smell good. Charlotte would have to walk very fast if she was going to be back in time for dinner. But thinking of dinner and smelling the chicken made her feel very hungry *now*. Very quietly she took the tin from the cupboard and put some sugar cookies into her apron pocket alongside her clothespin doll. The doll's pretty dress was finished, but she still did not have a name. Charlotte stood on tiptoe to reach her Sunday bonnet on its peg by the door. She tied its red laces all by herself and slipped out of the house.

She crossed Tide Mill Lane and cut between the trees behind the smithy, coming out onto Washington Street just across from the gristmill. The mill's big wooden wheel turned around in the swift waters of Stony

Brook, and the millpond lay flat and gray beyond it. Charlotte crossed Stony Brook on the bridge and followed the road toward the center of town.

The road was busy with carts, some pulled by horses and some by oxen. The drivers touched their hats and nodded at Charlotte, and Charlotte remembered to curtsy each time. The proud, gleaming horses made a brisk *clop-clop* sound, and the burly oxen made a heavy *clump-clump, clump-clump*. Their hooves left dents in the soft dirt of the road.

Walking to Boston took a long time. Charlotte ate one cookie and then she ate two more. That left three cookies, and she supposed she had better save them for the walk home. Mama said you must never take the food or drink the fairies offered you, or you would be trapped in fairyland for a hundred years or more. Charlotte hoped it would not take long to reach Scotland, once she got to Boston. Surely it was getting close to dinner-time now. Without thinking about it, she nibbled on another cookie. A yellow dog trotted out of a lane and fell into step beside her. It looked up at her with friendly eyes and an open mouth, as if to say, *Good day, miss. I could use a nibble too*. Charlotte sighed and broke off a bit of cookie for it. It was not polite to eat in front of others without sharing, even dogs.

She came to the wide, shop-lined square that was the town common, where the meeting-house was, and the new town hall. After that she passed a lot of shops and houses, and several streets that ran into Washington Street. She had not known Washington Street was so long. Through her bonnet the sun felt hot on the top of her head.

"I'm going to Boston," she told the yellow dog. The dog gave a cheerful bark and turned off down a lane, wagging its tail as it trotted away.

"Oh!" Charlotte said. "Good-bye then." Without the dog she felt a little lonely. There were many people about, ladies in their rib-boned bonnets with baskets over their arms, farmers in tall straw hats and homespun shirts, young men in pantaloons laughing in doorways. But none of them paid Charlotte any mind, and that made her feel lonelier.

She put her hand in her apron pocket and squeezed her clothespin doll. Charlotte had been thinking very hard about a name since her birthday, but she had not decided on one yet. Mama said choosing a name was like choosing a good boughten cloth: You must choose something that would wear well and fit the wearer, for it must last a long time.

Lydia had a rag doll that she had named three times. First it had been called Anna Clarice, after the minister's wife. Then Mary had been born and Lydia had changed her doll's name to Mary too. But after a while that got too confusing and Lydia changed it to Rachel. Mama said Rachel was a fine name and Lydia ought to let it stand.

Charlotte thought about all the names she knew. Mama's name was Martha. Will's sweetheart was named Lucy. Mr. Stowe, the cooper, had three daughters named Anne, Jane, and Hannah. They were all very pretty names, but none of them seemed right for the little rosy-cheeked doll in her blue-plaid dress.

All the time she was thinking about this, Charlotte was looking for the Neck. Lydia had said there was water on both sides of the road, like crossing a bridge. Seagulls squawked overhead—that meant water was nearby. But Charlotte walked and walked and did not see a big water. Into the back of her mind crept a small worry that she had not brought enough cookies for the trip.

She came to a marshy place where there were no houses or shops. On both sides of the road the wet ground was studded with clumps of stringy grass and tall, velvety stands of cattails pointing stubbornly at the sky. There was a damp, salty smell to the air. There were small pools and rivulets of water in places, but the road did not cross over these, and so this could not be the Neck.

The air was alive with an endless caterwaul of waterbirds. Someone had built a fence on both sides of the road. A gull perched on a

fence post and called out to Charlotte as she passed. A wood duck stared at her with its round eyes; its funny, flat-topped head shone green as a jewel. With a sudden rustle of wings two herons lifted up into the air. The strong wings flapped hard, and the long, pointed beaks seemed to slice through the sky. The spindly legs stuck out beneath the blue-gray bodies.

Far ahead Charlotte could see some houses spread out upon a hill. She had not known there were so many houses in Roxbury. She watched the houses come closer and closer as she walked.

A coach came toward her, pulled by two great horses. The driver tipped his hat to Charlotte as he went by. She wanted to ask him how far it was to Boston, but she did not dare. As the coach went past, she caught a glimpse of a face looking out through the small square window: a little boy with curled yellow hair beneath a blue sailor hat. He stared at Charlotte as he passed, looking very pleased with himself. Charlotte watched the coach rumble away. She wished she could ride in a coach like that.

Then a cart came toward her, pulled by two placid oxen. The cart was loaded high with sacks and packages, and a man walked beside it. The man wore a stained leather apron and a worn flannel cap. It looked just like Papa's cap and apron, and when the man got closer, he looked at Charlotte in surprise. It *was* Papa.

"Charlotte, lass!" Papa cried. "Whatever are ye doin' here, child?" He stopped the oxen. They stared at her with their sorrowful brown eyes. Papa strode quickly to Charlotte.

Charlotte did not say anything. She was surprised to see him; she had had no idea that Papa had gone to Boston this morning. The thought came to her all of a sudden that perhaps Papa and Mama would not be pleased she had come so far by herself. But she was very glad to see Papa all the same.

Papa's blue eyes were full of questions. "Do ye ken where ye are, lass? Ye're not a stone's throw from Boston!"

This was puzzling. She had yet not come to the place where the water touched the road, and she knew that place was the Neck and the Neck was a mile long. No one could throw a stone a whole mile, not even Papa.

"This is no place for a wee lass on her own," Papa said. His voice was grave. He squatted down and squeezed Charlotte's shoulders. "Where did ye think ye was goin', child?"

"To Scotland, Papa," said Charlotte. She explained about the fairies, and how she was going to Boston to look for the bridge that would take her over the sea to Scotland, where the fairies lived.

Papa's slow smile spread across his face. "Ah, lass," he said, "ye'll no make it tae Scotland this day, I fear. 'Tis a sight farther than you realize. Your mama and I, we sailed on ships to come to this country. Three months on board, I was, and your mither's journey was nearly half a year!"

Charlotte's heart fell. Her eyes felt like crying, and her throat felt too tight to talk. But she must talk, she must get Papa to explain everything to her. Nothing was as she had expected it to be. She would never get to Scotland to see the fairies. She had not even made it to Boston, for all it was so close.

"Dinna cry," Papa said. Charlotte *did* cry then. Between sobs she choked out a question.

"What's the sea, Papa? I thought it was a big water like Stony Brook."

"Like Stony—" Papa raised his eyes heavenward and whistled. "Have ye really lived your whole life a mile frae the sea withoot knowin' what it is? 'Tis a great wide stretch o' water, bigger than anything ye can imagine. Look, there—" he said, pointing eastward across the flats. "That's South Boston Bay, across there. A bay is a place where the sea cozies up tae the land. When the tide is in, the bay fills up all this place wi' seawater."

"Oh!" Charlotte said. She felt very much surprised. "Is this the Neck, Papa?"

"Aye," Papa said. "And those are the streets of Boston just ahead of ye, there. Ye came a great way on your own." His eyes were solemn now, and a little stern. "Ye're a plucky lass, Lottie, but ye're not to come this way again, mind. The Neck is no place for a girl your age on her own."

"Yes, Papa," she whispered. She could not help but stare at the houses she had seen scattered on the hillside in front of her. She had been looking right at Boston and had not known it.

Papa lifted Charlotte in his arms and carried her to the oxcart. "I can walk, Papa," Charlotte said, so Papa put her down, and she walked alongside him as he guided the oxen toward home with his long stick. It was Mr. Waitt's oxcart and oxen; Papa had borrowed them in exchange for repairing the ox chains and the axle.

Every few steps Charlotte looked back over her shoulder and saw the houses of Boston grow smaller. She felt silly, now, to think that she had thought she could make it all the way to Scotland and back before dinner. But it was not her fault no one had told her how big the sea was.

Great Hill

Back at home Mama scolded Charlotte and said she must never go near the Neck alone. "You might wander off in the flats and lose yourself," Mama said. "I should hate to think what would happen if you got caught out in the marshes wi' the tide comin' in."

"Yes, ma'am," Charlotte said. She felt disappointed; she would have liked to go back at high tide and see the sea licking at the fence posts. But she knew Mama meant what she said, and so she promised to stay away from the Neck and the salt marsh.

The chicken was sliced and on the table already. A warm smell of fried potatoes hung in the air, and steam rose from a bowl of mashed squash. There was a dish of pickled cauliflower and another filled with a golden quivering mass of pumpkin preserves made last fall. Mama told Charlotte to wash up and hurry to the table. Lydia had had to take the plates out of the cupboard herself because Charlotte had not been there. Mama said Charlotte must wipe all the dishes after dinner and put them away herself for a whole week, as punishment.

"Aye, that's just," Papa said, nodding gravely. "You stay close by your mither this afternoon and be a good lass. But when the clock strikes four, come to the smithy." He would not say what for. Charlotte wondered about it all through dinner, and she wondered even harder as she wiped the dishes afterward and put them in the cupboard. She saw now that she had been naughty this morning, and so it was not likely to be something nice waiting for her in the smithy. But she didn't think it could be anything too bad, either. Papa and Mama did not seem angry, only stern, and they had already given her a punishment.

At last it was four o'clock. Lydia walked with her to the smithy, holding Charlotte's hand. She said it was to keep her company, but Charlotte suspected Lydia only wanted to know what the surprise was. After all, Lydia had certainly not felt it necessary to "keep Charlotte company" while Charlotte did kitchen chores all the long afternoon.

Slowly Charlotte stepped out of the bright sun into the cool, dim shop. Papa smiled when he saw her, and Charlotte knew at once that the something that was waiting for her was going to be nice after all.

"Well, lads," Papa said to Will and Lewis and Tom, "I want ye tae come along too. We'll close the shop airly, this once."

Charlotte and Lydia looked at each other. This was exciting. Papa led them across the lane to the house. Mama was out in the garden with Mary, and Papa called to her.

Everyone must come, he said.

Mama's eyes lit up, and she snatched off her apron. She loved surprises. She lifted Mary to her hip and ran to catch up. Charlotte laughed to see Mama running like a little girl.

Papa led the way down the lane toward Washington Street. As they drew near the wide road, Mama slowed down and straightened her skirts. Her cheeks were flushed and her blue eyes danced. She grinned at Papa.

"You might have given me some warning," she scolded. "Me wi' me oldest dress on and no bonnet!"

"We're not going anywhere sae fancy," Papa said, with a twinkle in his eye. He strode calmly across Washington Street, lifting his hat to a lady and gentleman riding past in a large-wheeled buggy. The lady's eyes widened at the sight of Papa's sooty face and hands, and the even sootier faces and hands of Will and the boys, and Mama with nothing on her head but her plain linen cap. The lady's mouth pursed up in an "In-*deed!*" kind of way, and Mama laughed again.

"I canna blame her," she said as the buggy rolled past. "Never in me life have I seen such a raggle-taggle crew as we are today!"

Charlotte hurried to keep up with Papa. Lewis ran ahead so he could be first to get where they were going, but he didn't know where that was, and so he had to keep looking back over his shoulder to make sure everyone was still behind him.

"That way," Papa told him, pointing, and they followed a path that took them to Great Hill. That was a big hill that rose behind Mr. Ebenezer Craft's farm. Charlotte had seen Great Hill every day of her life, but she had never climbed it. Papa said she would climb it now.

Houses dotted the hillside, and higher up a rail fence cut across it like a collar. Four or five cows grazed on the slope. A great black crow sat surveying the world in the top of an oak tree, cawing in a harsh, proud voice that was even bigger than its own self.

"Why, look, Charlotte," Will said, "there's

the corbie's friend, come to see how the pickings are in America." For Charlotte had told him all about the corbie and the crow from Mama's song.

"Why aren't there any corbies in America?" Charlotte asked.

"Well, I suppose birds are like people. There's some kinds of birds that never leave the place where they were born. And there's others that travel the world, looking for the best spot to build their nest."

"Like Mama and Papa!"

"That's right."

They had come to the top of the hill. Papa said, "Now turn aroond and look. There's where you were today, Lottie."

Charlotte looked down at the bumpy tops of trees and the stark angles of rooftops. Beyond them was spread a vast field of blue. A dark line cut across the blue, and Papa said that was the Neck. The tide had come in, and seawater had filled in all that marshy space she had seen this morning. The road was the only dry place left.

It was strange to think she had been on that very road today. If someone had been standing here on Great Hill looking down, he could have seen Charlotte. The thought gave her a little creeping thrill down her spine.

On the other side of the watery blue field were small dots and smudges that Papa said were the buildings of Boston. They speckled a round slope that was the same hill Charlotte had seen from the road. Papa pointed to a glint of gold against the pale-blue sky. That was the dome of the State House, he said, which the famous Mr. Paul Revere and his brother had covered with copper.

Then Papa pointed to the east. Away out there the blue of the water melted into the blue of the sky. You could not tell where the water ended. Papa said it did not end; it stretched on and on for more miles than Charlotte could imagine. He pointed to a black speck in the blue and said that was a ship, a British frigate probably, part of the blockade.

Mama put Mary down to crawl in the grass.

Lydia sat down beside her and began picking small white-petaled oxeyes for a daisy chain. Tom and Lewis began a game of ships and ran about pretending to fire their cannons upon each other.

But Charlotte only stood there staring at the glittering blue edge of the sea. That edge was the beginning of a water as big as half a year. Far, far on the other side was Scotland, the green country where Mama and Papa had lived. Not even fairy magic could make a person's eyes see across that distance.

On School Street

O n the first Monday in June Charlotte put on her blue linen dress and the new white muslin apron. The dress had gotten too short, so Mama had added a ruffle to the bottom. Charlotte liked to look down and see the crisp edge of her apron and the ruffle sticking out beneath. The apron had two pockets. Into the left one Charlotte put her clothespin doll. Tomorrow, she promised the apron, she would put the doll on the other side. Neither pocket must be made to feel left out.

"And I must think of a name for you, poor thing," she told the doll.

Mama had made Tom put on his new blue shirt with the buttons on the bottom that fastened onto his pantaloons. The buttons curved over Tom's round stomach in a wide half-circle that was exactly like the frown on his face. Tom hated wearing his button-up pantaloons.

"Not the jacket too!" he begged, but Mama was firm. Gloomily he pulled on the jacket, and he stood fidgeting with his collar while Mama combed his hair.

He was somewhat consoled, however, by the special breakfast Mama had made, of boiled beef and eggs. Afterward Mama gave Tom their dinner basket packed with bread and cheese and some ginger cookies, all wrapped in a red-and-white-checked napkin. Charlotte longed to carry the basket. But Mama said Tom must carry it to school, and Charlotte could carry it home.

Charlotte had her own schoolbook to carry to school, though. It was scuffed and worn, for

Tom had used it, and Lydia, and Lewis. It had a yellow cover with the letters P-R-I-M-E-R on it in black. Mama told her they spelled "Primer," and that a primer was a book for learning to read.

Charlotte felt proud to have her own schoolbook. Last year she hadn't had one; she had been too little.

Tom had his book too, a slim brown one that had water spots on the cover, from a puddle that Lewis had splashed in when he was only seven, the age Tom was now. Tom threw the book into the basket on top of the napkin.

"The cookies!" Charlotte cried. "You'll break them to bits."

But Tom only shrugged and said, "Won't make them taste any different."

"They will," Charlotte insisted. Tom just stuck out his tongue, and Charlotte sighed.

"You're older than me," she said. "You ought to have more sense."

Their path took them along Washington Street to Stony Brook. They passed Mr. Waitt's gristmill, where, through the open door, Charlotte and Tom could see the heavy mill-stones turning and turning, grinding a stream of grain into flour.

Tom liked the mill almost as much as he liked Papa's smithy. Forgetting to be grumpy about his jacket and his buttons, he swung the dinner basket around in the air like the millwheel. Charlotte felt nearly frantic thinking about the cookies.

"Come *on*, Tom," she said, hurrying past the mill.

They turned onto Centre Street, a broad, rutted road that skirted Stony Brook. Wood lilies blazed orange-red at the roadside. On the bank were clusters of harebells bobbing on their delicate stalks, the bells blue as little bits of sky.

They went around a curve in the road, and there, just ahead of them, was their teacher. Her name was Miss Heath, and she was their neighbor. The windows of their house looked out upon Miss Heath's father's land, but his big white house was hidden behind a hill.

As far back as Charlotte could remember, Miss Heath had come calling with her mother, Mrs. John Heath, to spend snowy afternoons sewing in Mama's cozy parlor. But Miss Heath had been just Amelia then. Mama said it seemed only yesterday that Amelia was a little red-cheeked girl Lydia's age, with her braids flying every which way.

But now she was a grown-up lady of seventeen who wore her hair piled on top of her head, and Charlotte must remember to call her "Miss Heath."

Miss Heath taught school only in the summers. The winter term was taught by a schoolmaster who came down from Boston. Charlotte had heard frightening stories about how he whipped children or made them stand in the freezing corner farthest from the fireplace when they did not know their lessons. She was very glad she did not yet have to go to school in the winter. Miss Heath was much nicer.

Charlotte said good day and made a curtsy. It was a very good curtsy and she felt quite proud. Amelia—Miss Heath—would see that Charlotte had grown up a great deal, now that she was five years old. Tom bowed solemnly, staring at the teacher with his round eyes. He was always bashful around ladies. Charlotte thought with some satisfaction that now he would not be able to swing the dinner basket around.

Miss Heath smiled at them and said good day. She wore a green bonnet trimmed with ribbons and flowers, and over her ruffled muslin gown she wore a short, lacy jacket called a spencer. She was pretty and plump, with tendrils of black hair peeping out from under her bonnet.

"Shall we walk together?" she asked. She held out her hand for Charlotte to hold. Charlotte was suddenly glad she did not have to carry the basket. She was so proud to be walking to school with her teacher that she quite forgot she had not wanted to go to school this summer.

The district schoolhouse was on School Street. Its unpainted clapboard walls had weathered to every shade of brown. Inside was an entryway with pegs for coats in winter and a shelf where Tom stowed the dinner basket next to lots of other baskets.

An open doorway led to the large schoolroom. In the front of the room was a raised platform upon which sat Miss Heath's desk. There was a fireplace on one wall, clean and empty now for summer. The other three walls were lined with rough wooden desks, bearing scars and ink stains from the pupils of years past. The high benches that went with the desks had no backs, so that the students could sit facing either way—toward the desks and walls, or into the center of the room. The desks were for the older students, and Tom took a seat at one of them next to some other boys his age.

Charlotte wasn't sure where she belonged. In the middle of the room were a few more rows of benches that had no desks. These were reserved for the very youngest children; they were crowded now with three- and four-year-olds, and even one chubby two-year-old named Simon Griggs, whose mother had sent him to school to keep him out from underfoot during the busy summer months.

They were called the abecedarians, for they did not study anything but the ABC. They squirmed and fidgeted on the benches. They did not yet know they were supposed to keep quiet in school, and they talked and cried and made a terrible racket. Some of them had older sisters who kept *shhh*ing from the outside benches.

Charlotte recalled how she had been an abecedarian the year before. The bench had been so high that her feet hadn't touched the floor, and her dangling legs had ached dreadfully. All day long she had been expected to sit still on the bench and not fall asleep. Every once in a while Miss Heath had gone over the ABC with them, but mostly she had been too busy trying to keep order among the older students. Charlotte had learned a few of the letters, but she could not remember the whole alphabet.

She was afraid she would have to sit with

the center-bench babies again. But Miss Heath told her she belonged in an outside row, with the primer class. There were two other children in that class: a thin, shaggy-haired boy who shared a bench with his older brother, and a girl Charlotte's age sitting all by herself.

"Sit there beside Susan, Charlotte," Miss Heath said, pointing to the empty spot beside the girl. Charlotte sat with the desk behind her, facing into the center of the room, like the rest of the older children. The school-house was crowded this summer; more than half of the outside benches were full.

Charlotte saw a great many children whom she knew from church, or from school last summer, or from calling on neighbors with Mama. But she had never before seen the girl beside her. Susan, Miss Heath had called her. While Miss Heath made a short welcom-ing speech, Charlotte tried to steal a look at her seatmate without letting on that she was doing so. All she got was a glimpse of very clean apron over faded pink calico, and the sudden impression that the girl was openly studying her. Quickly Charlotte looked away and pretended to be listening to Miss Heath with all her might.

But after Miss Heath had said the morning prayer, the girl whispered to Charlotte, "I have a plum tart in my dinner basket. You can have some if you like."

"Oh!" said Charlotte, surprised. "You can have some of my cookies," she added hastily so the girl wouldn't think she was greedy. "Only I think they're all broken up."

"That's all right," Susan whispered. "They taste *almost* as good that way."

"Yes, *almost*," Charlotte said, and she smiled. She knew all at once that they were going to be friends—for here was someone who understood that broken cookies did not taste quite as good as whole ones.

At dinnertime they found a spot together on the grassy slope beside the schoolhouse, beneath a stand of silvery birches. Tom came running up and made impatient noises while Charlotte unfolded the red-and-white napkin.

"Hurry up," he said crossly. "The other fellows will be done eating by the time I get there."

He snatched up his share of the bread and cheese. Beneath them was a jumble of broken cookies.

Charlotte glared at Tom reproachfully. He shrugged as if to say it didn't matter, but his eyes looked sorry.

"Here," he said carelessly, "this one is almost whole. You can have it."

He picked out his share of cookie pieces and ran off to join the other boys his age, calling back over his shoulder, "Don't throw out the crumbs—I'll eat 'em later!"

Charlotte rolled her eyes. But Susan laughed and said, "You're awfully lucky to have a brother."

"Don't you?" Charlotte asked.

"No, nor any sisters either," the girl said. Charlotte felt a bit taken aback. She couldn't think of anyone else she knew who was the only child in the family. Who did Susan play with? Charlotte felt suddenly very glad to have so many brothers and sisters—even a brother like Tom, who would as soon eat a pile of crumbs off a napkin as a nice, whole, round cookie.

"I'd give anything for a sister," Susan said. "If I had one, her name would be Emmeline."

"Oh, how lovely!" said Charlotte.

Susan had brown eyes and silky brown hair, straight as a pin, that she wore tucked behind her ears. When she laughed, which was often, her hair slipped out and fell into her eyes. Her whole name was Susan Custer.

"The boys at my old school called me 'Susan Custard,'" she confided. "But my mama told me it's a compliment, because custard is so nice and sweet and everybody likes it."

Charlotte didn't know what a compliment was, but she knew that she liked Susan Custer very much.

"I think you're nicer than custard," she said frankly.

Susan beamed at her. "And *you're* nicer than—than peppermints!"

Susan, it turned out, was a great expert on peppermints. Her father was a merchant who owned three ships. He used to bring home peppermints and other candies all the time. But now, Susan told Charlotte importantly, times were hard for him because of the war.

"It's the blockade," she explained. Charlotte nodded solemnly. Susan told her that his ships had been docked for months, because the British navy would not let them out of Boston Harbor. Until last week Susan had lived in Boston, but now her family had come to stay with her uncle on Centre Street. He was a tinsmith, and Susan's father had come to work in his shop.

"While his ships rot at harbor," said Susan. Rotting ships sounded like a terrible thing to Charlotte, but it was clear that Susan was rather proud of it.

Miss Heath came out then and rang the bell. Reluctantly Susan and Charlotte stood and folded up their napkins. It was so pleasant sitting out in the speckled shade of the birches, amid the soft grass and the yellow dandelions, bright as suns.

But it was nice sitting next to each other in the schoolroom, too. Susan did not have a primer to study from, so Charlotte said she would share hers. She held it half on her lap and half on Susan's so they could both see.

Miss Heath told them to study the first two pages. There was a verse at the top, and below it was the ABC, each letter in a little box with a picture and a word that went with it. Miss Heath read them the verse and said they must learn it by heart before the end of the week.

It went:

> *He that ne'er learns his A, B, C,*
> *For ever will a Blockhead be;*
> *But he that learns these Letters fair*
> *Shall have a Coach to take the Air.*

They repeated it two or three times after Miss Heath, until they began to know it by heart. Then she left them and said she must give Freddy Tanner his lesson. He was the shaggy-haired boy in the primer class with them, but he studied from a different book.

While Miss Heath was with Freddy, Charlotte and Susan had to sit still and be quiet. They stared at the pictures below their verse. Charlotte knew the names of some of the letters, and she thought she could see how they went with the words and pictures. *A for Apple, B for Bull, C for Cat.*

Then Miss Heath went over to the other side of the room to give an arithmetic lesson to Tom's class. Charlotte and Susan stared at the primer as if they were studying, and whispered to each other.

They agreed that the verse at the top of the page was some of the finest poetry they had ever heard.

"I wonder when we'll get our coach," Susan said.

"Oh!" said Charlotte. "Do you think we'll really get one?" She had not thought about whether the verse was true or not.

"Of course we will," said Susan confidently. "You don't think they'd let us study with a book that *lied*, do you?"

"Why, no, I guess not," Charlotte faltered. When Susan put it that way, it made great sense. Mama would not give her any book that told falsehoods.

"But," she said, puzzling it out, "Tom knows his ABC, and he doesn't have a coach. Nor Lydia nor Lewis. My Mama and Papa don't even have one, and they know how to read."

"Mine too," said Susan, "but they didn't study from this book." She tucked her hair behind her ears, thinking it over. "I don't know about your brothers and sister. They aren't blockheads, are they?"

"Of course not!" Charlotte cried. She forgot to whisper. Miss Heath looked up sharply.

"Girls," she said, in a voice that was all Miss Heath—there was not a trace of Amelia in it.

That was the end of whispering for that afternoon.

But after school they walked together as far as Centre Street. Tom ran on ahead. He was glad not to have to wait for Charlotte.

Charlotte was glad too. She didn't want to

talk about the coach in front of Tom. She could not understand why he hadn't been given one, nor Lydia and Lewis. The verse said plain as plain that anyone who learned his letters should "have a Coach to take the Air."

"Perhaps," she said, "it only means taking a ride in one."

The more she and Susan talked about it, the more they longed to ride in a coach. To sit high above the great black wheels behind a team of horses—black ones, perhaps, with glossy manes and braided tails and a prancing walk—looking out a little square window at the streets rolling past—what could be finer? How proud their mothers would be!

Charlotte remembered the boy she had seen in the coach that had passed her on the road to Boston. He had looked very pleased with himself, in his blue sailor hat and collar. Perhaps *he* had just learned his ABC. Perhaps she and Susan would be given a ride in that very same coach.

She decided not to say anything about it at

home. It was to be a surprise for Mama and Papa. Some afternoon they would hear wheels crunching over the gravel of Tide Mill Lane, and Lewis would run to the window and holler, "By gum!" The driver would climb to the ground and offer a hand to help Charlotte out of the shining black carriage. Lydia would stare and Mama would clap. Tom, of course, would know about it already, having had to trudge home on foot behind the coach.

Long before the week was out, both girls knew the verse by heart. Miss Heath called them to the front of the room and made them recite it to the class. They both got through it perfectly—even with Tom making faces at them from his seat, and little Simon Griggs in the front row tumbling off his bench halfway through.

The next day Miss Heath said they must learn the rest of the page. When they knew all the letters and the words that went with them, they would stand up and recite those.

"And after that," Susan said on the way home, "the coach is sure to come."

C for Coach

During the next week there was far less whispering on Charlotte and Susan's bench than there might otherwise have been. The girls bent over the primer, their two heads close enough to touch, staring hard at the letters and the helpful pictures that went with each one. *D for Dog, E for Egg*, Charlotte mouthed silently, and Susan's lips moved noiselessly behind the curtain of her hair.

At last came the day when Miss Heath called them up to recite. Charlotte and Susan squeezed each other's hands. They went to stand beside the teacher's desk. Freddy Tanner came too.

"Charlotte, you first," said Miss Heath.

Charlotte took a deep breath. Her stomach felt fluttery. She hated to stand up here with everyone staring at her.

"A for Apple," she began. She made it all the way to "J for Judge" without any difficulty, but then she caught a glimpse of Abner Dickinson in the back of the room. He was gaping at her with his eyes crossed and his mouth twisted into a hideous grimace. It was such an ugly face that Charlotte's mind went blank for a moment. She knew what letter came next—she *did* know it—but that face!

Then Tom saw what Abner was doing and socked him on the shoulder. Tom might make all the faces he liked at his own sister, but no one else had better try it.

Charlotte smiled at him gratefully. "K for King," she said, because of course she had known it all along.

"L for Lion, M for Mouse, N for Nag." She

did not falter again until "Y," which always stumped her because the picture in the book did not, in her opinion, make any sense.

She closed her eyes hard and saw the picture in her mind. It was a lamb, but she must not say "Y for Lamb"; that was not it. . . .

"Y for Young Lamb!" she cried triumphantly. That was it. As if there was any such thing as an *old* lamb!

"And Z for Zany," she finished. The picture for that one was a court jester, with bells on his hat. Charlotte could see it clearly in her mind's eye, and she felt as if the bells were ringing for her, for she had made it all the way through! This afternoon the coach would come for her and she would ride home grand as a queen.

If, that was, Susan got through her ABC too. For Charlotte could not think of "taking the air" in the coach without her.

Susan did get through. There was one terrifying moment when she came to a dead stop and her eyes looked wild. Charlotte had to bite her lip to stop herself from calling out what came next. But at last Susan gulped and gave a little jump, and the words burst out of her.

"X for Xerxes!" That was the one Susan always had the most trouble with; she had often complained to Charlotte that the crowned man in the drawing could be any old king, and that his name might just as easily have been George or John as Xerxes. But she had remembered at last, and her voice soared as she finished. "Y for Young Lamb—Z FOR ZANY!"

"Goodness," Miss Heath said, blinking. "Very good, Susan, but you must remember that a young lady never shouts."

"Yes, ma'am!" Susan said, in a voice that stopped just short of being a shout itself. Charlotte grinned at her; she was so glad that both of them had made it through.

Then it was Freddy's turn. His book had different pictures for the letters. Charlotte thought it must not have been a very good book, for Freddy got only as far as S before stumbling to a stop.

"Don't know the rest," he mumbled.

"You must study harder, Frederick," said Miss Heath. "You may try again tomorrow."

Charlotte felt a stab of guilt. She felt sorry for Freddy, truly she did. But she was a little glad that now she could ride alone in the coach with Susan.

She followed Susan and Freddy back to their seats. When they slid onto their bench, Susan beamed at her.

"How will we ever wait till school is out?" Charlotte asked. "I don't think I can bear it."

"Nor I," Susan agreed.

But bear it they did. At last the long day was over, and Miss Heath said, "Class is dismissed." Charlotte half expected her to say something about the coach, but she supposed Miss Heath was keeping it quiet out of consideration for Freddy's feelings.

"Let's wait on the steps," she told Susan.

They waited and waited. All the other children left, but the coach did not appear.

After a while Miss Heath came out of the schoolhouse, tying on her bonnet.

"Why, girls! Did you wish to speak with me?"

"No, ma'am," said Susan. "We're waiting to take the air."

"I beg your pardon?" Miss Heath asked.

"In the *coach*," Susan explained.

Miss Heath's brow was furrowed. Charlotte could see that she did not understand at all. Carefully she repeated for her teacher the verse from the primer.

"We *did* learn 'these Letters fair,'" she said, "but the coach hasn't come."

"Oh, my dears," said Miss Heath, and her eyes were very kind. "I'm afraid you have misunderstood. That's only poetry—it's meant to inspire you, you see."

Charlotte didn't see, but she was too polite to say so. Miss Heath went on for quite some time about "forming good habits" and "working hard being its own reward" and "going far in life." At last she stopped and said gently, "Don't feel bad. I can see you're disappointed, but you oughtn't to let it spoil your success. It's a grand thing to know one's alphabet."

"Yes, ma'am," Charlotte murmured. It did not feel very grand. She took Susan's hand, and they said good-bye to Miss Heath. Together they went down the steps and through the dooryard to School Street.

A lump came into Charlotte's throat. There would be no coach ride. No glossy, proudly trotting horses; no little square window to look out of. They walked along slowly, their shadows stretching ahead of them on the road.

"Look," Charlotte said suddenly. "Our shadows. They're like grown-up ladies."

"Oh!" Susan cried. "They are! Only the skirts are too short. Grown-up ladies would wear longer skirts."

"And bonnets," Charlotte admitted. But it was still fun to watch the shadows and pretend they were themselves, all grown up. It almost—but not quite—took their minds off the coach.

"When I'm grown up," Charlotte declared, "I'm going to have a coach all my own. I'll drive around all day and give rides to little girls who know their lessons."

"Will your husband let you?" Susan asked.

"He'll have to," said Charlotte. "Or I won't let *him* ride in it. And another thing," she added suddenly. "I'm going to fix all the schoolbooks." She kicked at a stone and watched it skitter down the road. "So that they don't tell *falsehoods*."

"Oh, Charlotte, that's a lovely plan," said Susan admiringly. She smiled at Charlotte and locked arms with her. On the road their shadows locked arms too, tall and slender and graceful as ladies.

Emmeline

One July day a mysterious thing happened. School was going along as usual; it was a hot, stifling, noisy afternoon. Miss Heath was calling out exercises for Tom's class to write in their copybooks. It was slow going, for she had to stop every few words to wait while someone cut a new point on a quill pen or cleaned up a spill of ink. Each time she stopped, the little children in the front row let loose a flurry of questions—"May I go out?"—"Please, may I eat?"—"I want to go home!"—and on and on until Miss Heath began to look as if she'd like to go home herself.

The other classes were supposed to be studying lessons in their readers. Charlotte had stared at the long rows of words in her book—*bed, bid, big, bit*—until her eyes blurred. She longed to stretch out on the bench and go to sleep, like little Simon Griggs in the front row. Simon lay with his cheek pressed against the bench and one arm dangling over the side, not at all disturbed by a muffled quarrel taking place over his head between two of his schoolmates. Every now and then Miss Heath directed a loud "Hush!" toward the two small boys, who were fighting over a dead worm that had been found on the steps at dinner. One of the boys held the worm clutched so tightly in his fist that Charlotte wondered if there would be anything left of it by the time the quarrel was over.

Susan had given up studying altogether and was staring dreamily across the room and out the window. Suddenly she cried out in surprise. Her voice cut through the classroom hum. Everyone turned to look at her; Miss Heath's eyebrows made questioning points on her brow.

"What is it, Susan?"

"I—I beg your pardon," Susan stammered. "It's just that I saw my cousin Frank coming— and here he is."

And indeed, a young man had just entered the room, ducking his head apologetically. He glanced at Susan and then hurried to speak to Miss Heath. Miss Heath's puzzled expression changed to one of concern, and she too looked toward Susan and quickly away.

"Yes, indeed, I'll see to it," she told the young man. He thanked her and strode back toward the door, giving Susan a little wave as he went.

Susan's eyes were wide and bewildered. She waited for Miss Heath to explain. Charlotte felt her own heart beating with worry— suppose something had happened? Things did happen sometimes. Mothers took sick, fathers fell off ladders or got knocked down by angry bulls . . . but of course Susan's father was not a farmer, so he wouldn't be likely to run afoul of any bulls, angry or otherwise. Perhaps—the thought leaped into her mind—perhaps something had happened to one of his ships, up at the harbor in Boston. . . .

But all Miss Heath said was "Susan, your cousin says you're to go home with Charlotte this afternoon. Charlotte's mother is expecting you. You shall stay there all night, dear, and in the morning your father will send word what you are to do."

Susan and Charlotte looked at each other in disbelief. This was certainly nothing Charlotte would have guessed. How lovely to think of having Susan spend the night in her house! But it was odd, too, and she could see that Susan was worried.

"Please, ma'am," Susan asked, "is anything wrong?"

Miss Heath paused a moment, then shook her head. She would not say anything more about it, except to tell Susan not to worry and that her father would explain everything tomorrow.

After that the day dragged on even more slowly than it had before. Miss Heath finished calling out exercises to Tom's class and told them to copy out each sentence five times, and to mind their penmanship. Then she went around looking at the sewing samplers of the girls in the second and third classes.

"Your letters are beginning to run uphill, Hannah," she said, and "You've made that S backward, Ruthie. You must pick out the stitches and try it again." Charlotte listened with interest, wishing she were old enough to work on a sampler too. But Miss Heath was soon finished, and then there was only the second class's arithmetic lesson to listen to. Beside her on the bench Susan fidgeted impatiently.

It seemed as if surely a week must have passed when at last Miss Heath stood and said, "School is dismissed." Charlotte and Susan hurried out the door and down the road. They went so fast that Tom did not catch up to them until they reached the mill.

"Why are you running?" he asked, panting. "You left the dinner basket, Charlotte—I saw it on my way out."

"Oh!" Charlotte had forgotten all about the basket. She didn't know why they were running, exactly, only that it seemed important to get home quickly.

"Do you think your mother will know what's happened?" Susan asked.

Tom shrugged. "It's likely. She knows most everything that's going on. Maybe your house burned down," he added helpfully.

Susan gasped, and her eyes looked frantic. "Tom!" cried Charlotte angrily. She grabbed Susan's hand, and together they sprinted past the smithy and across Tide Mill Lane to the house. Mama and Lydia were out beside the garden wall, folding up linen sheets that had been spread out to bleach in the sun all day. Mary stood holding on to the wall nearby, her long white frock trailing in the dirt.

Charlotte and Susan ran to Mama and pulled at her dress, speaking both at once. Mama laughed and told them to calm down.

Then she put a hand on Susan's head and said, "Dinna work yourself into a lather, lass. Your papa was here not an hour gone, and he said to tell you your mother's just a mite under the weather. We shall have us a grand time tonight, and in the mornin' he'll come for you."

Her smile was so warm that Charlotte did not feel worried anymore. Susan's house had not burned down, and her father's ships were safe.

"Will my mother be all right?" Susan asked, twisting her apron between her hands.

"You must do as your papa says, child, and not worry yourself," Mama said gently. Then she told them to run and play until tea.

Lydia said they might play graces with her stick-and-hoop set, if they took Mary with them. So Charlotte and Susan took Mary by the hands and, holding her gown out of the way, led her to a flat stretch of ground beyond the garden. Mary went on wobbly, stumbling legs, for she had only just begun to walk. Charlotte gave her the clothespin doll to play with.

"Now, you mustn't get her dress dirty," she warned sternly. Mary beamed and waved the doll around in the air.

The graces set had been a present on Lydia's last birthday. It was a small wooden hoop the size of a plate, and two sticks as long as Charlotte's arm.

Charlotte took one stick and Susan took the other. Holding the hoop on her stick, Charlotte took a few steps backward. She used the stick to toss the hoop through the air toward Susan, and Susan tried to catch it on her own stick. But the hoop flew right past her. Susan ran laughing to pick it up, and then she sailed it back to Charlotte on her own stick. It was tricky to catch the hoop with the thin sticks, and it made them laugh so much, they couldn't hold the sticks steady.

Suddenly Susan cried, "Mary, no!" and lunged toward the baby. Mary had the doll's head in her mouth and was sucking happily. Charlotte ran to rescue her poor doll from the sticky mouth, causing Mary to wail in outrage.

Anxiously Charlotte wiped the wet head with her apron.

"Mary, how could you!" she yelled. "If her face is gone . . ."

But it was all right. The paint had not rubbed off; the red mouth still smiled, and the black eyes stared as cheerfully as ever. There were only two little dents on the back of the glossy head to show that Mary had gotten at it.

"She left *bite* marks," Charlotte fumed.

"You can hardly see them," Susan said kindly. "It's lucky her hair is dark."

Mary wouldn't stop crying, so they took her back to Mama and Lydia. Mama lifted the baby to her hip and said, "There, there, my little one. You'll get on better in life if you learn not to eat other mothers' children."

That made everyone giggle. Charlotte kissed her doll and stroked her poor dented head.

"Aren't you *ever* going to name her?" Lydia asked.

"Of course I am!" Charlotte was indignant. "I just haven't found the perfect name yet."

Susan climbed up on top of the garden wall

and tried to walk around it. After a few steps she wobbled and fell off. It was all right, for the wall was low. Charlotte had fallen off it lots of times; but she almost never fell now, for she had had a lot of practice. She showed Susan how to stretch out her arms to keep her balance. The sun-warmed puddingstone felt hot on their bare feet.

"Why is it called puddingstone, Mama?" Charlotte asked.

"Whisht! Have I never told you that story?" Mama cried. "I canna believe it." She sat right down on the warm stone wall, with Mary in her lap, and told it to them.

Mama's Story about the Puddingstone

A long, long time ago there was a giant livin' here wi' his family. He was so big that the whole of Roxbury Common could fit in his front parlor.

This giant, he had him a wife and three children, a girl in the middle and a boy at each end. And these children—och!

You never saw such a spoiled lot in all your life. They wouldna do their chores, and they wouldna mind their manners, and they fought and they quarreled till even the sun couldna bear to listen and hid its face behind a cloud. Then the gray weather made them quarrel all the more.

Now at that time all this land was flat as flat could be. There wasna so much as a bump in the ground from here to Dorchester. The giants' feet were so broad, you see, and them so very heavy, that whatever they stepped on they crushed to powder. Where the children played not even grass could grow.

But one day the wife, she thought she'd give the children a treat for dinner. She mixed up a pudding, a lovely plummy pudding fit for a king. She brought it to the table and dished up a helping for each of her children.

The oldest child looked in the youngest child's bowl, and he cried out, "'Tisn't fair—you've given him more!"

So the giant's wife put a little more pudding in the oldest child's dish.

Then the middle child cried out, "'Tisn't fair—you've given him more!"

So the wife put a little more pudding in her dish.

Then the youngest cried out, "'Tisn't fair—you've given her more!"

And at that the wife gave up tryin' and plopped the pudding pan on the table.

"You may serve yourselves," she said, and she left the room.

The oldest child snatched up the pudding dish and put all the rest of the pudding in his own bowl. The other two children cried out in rage and grabbed for the bowl. The girl caught hold of one side, and the youngest, he caught hold of the other. And the three of them yanked and they tugged and they pulled that bowl back and forth between them. They pulled so hard that the bowl went flyin' out of all their hands and sailed right through the open window.

Now remember, this was a giant's bowl, and sure it was a giant's pudding. There was enough of it there to feed an army of folks like us. Pudding went this way and pudding went that way. You canna imagine the mess. From here to Dorchester the land was covered with lumps o' pudding. The bowl landed upside down right over yon, where Great Hill is, wi' a big mess o' pudding still clingin' to its sides.

Well, when the giant's wife saw the mess, she said she'd have no part in clearin' it away. The children had made it, and the children must clean it up. But those naughty children, they never did wipe up their mess, and so those lumps of pudding stayed where they were.

When night came, they cooled off, and by morning they were hard as stone. And there they stayed, year after year—and there they are today.

"Whenever someone like your Papa wants to build a wall," Mama finished, "all he has to do is find himself a good lump o' pudding."

"I know what Great Hill is!" Charlotte cried. "It's the upside-down bowl!"

"Aye," said Mama. "Away on the other side o' Great Hill there's a quarry, where folks have dug right through to the pudding inside. Roxbury puddingstone is known up and down New England, it is."

She looked at the sun burning in the tops of the maple trees. "Goodness, how late it's gettin'!" She said they must all go inside to put tea on the table.

Susan helped Charlotte take the plates out of the cupboard. Charlotte showed her the Saturday mother and father. It was lovely to have someone to share her secret with. The poor father jug was still empty, shoved back a little now into the dark corner of the cupboard. Charlotte pulled him toward the front, where he could at least keep company with the cookie tin.

That night was like a holiday, with Susan tucked in between Charlotte and Lydia in their bed, her hands covered up by the too-long sleeves of Lydia's last-year's nightgown. They whispered and giggled until Mama came in to say they were making so much noise, she had no doubt the cows were having trouble sleeping, out in the barn.

"Shall I sing you to sleep?" she asked. When they eagerly said yes, she brought her small flax wheel upstairs and sat spinning in the dim light of a single candle, singing a low, sweet song she had learned as a girl in Scotland.

> *"Come all ye men and maidens and list unto*
> *my rhyme,*
> *'Twas all about a damsel who was scarcely*
> *in her prime;*
> *She beat the blushin' roses and admired by*
> *all around*
> *Was lovely young Caroline of Edinboro*
> *Town."*

The candle flickered, and on the ceiling the shadow of a great wheel spun round and round. Charlotte lay watching it until her eyes closed, but still it seemed as if she could see the dark spokes revolving behind her eyelids. Mama's voice was soft as a kiss.

> *"Young Henry was a Highland man*
> *a-courtin' to her came,*
> *And when her parents came to know they did*
> *not like the same;*
> *Young Henry was offended and unto her did*
> *say,*
> *'Arise, my dearest Caroline, and with me*
> *run away.'"*

The next morning Susan was helping Charlotte wipe the breakfast dishes when her father burst into the kitchen.

"I beg your pardon, Mrs. Tucker," Mr. Custer panted. "That is— Good day. I—er— How do you do?"

He took off his hat and put it back on again, and then took it off and laid it absently on the table, in the middle of the floury spot where Mama had been rolling out a piecrust. He was a large, heavyset man who looked more like a farmer than a merchant, with his powerful arms and his shirtsleeves rolled up.

Mama smiled and greeted him warmly. She studied his face and said softly, "I trust all is well?"

Mr. Custer grinned broadly. "Indeed it is!" He went to Susan and caught her up in a bear hug. "And how's my little lady?" he asked. "Shall we go home and see who's come to visit your mama?"

"Who is it?" Susan asked, but Charlotte knew at once what he meant.

"A baby!" she cried. She remembered a distant time when Mrs. John Heath had come and taken Charlotte and Lydia and the boys to her big white house on the other side of the hill beyond the garden. Miss Heath—she had been Amelia then—had given Charlotte a doughnut to eat. Later Charlotte had been set atop a gray horse that stood quietly munching oats; and then Papa had come and told them all they had a new sister at home; and that was how Mary had come to live with them.

Charlotte dropped her dishcloth and

squeezed Susan's hand. "You're a big sister!"

"Truly?" Susan stared at her father.

Beaming, he nodded. "She's hit the nail on the head, Charlotte has. Clever girl!"

"Oh, Papa!" cried Susan, clasping her hands. "What is her name to be? Oh, please, might we call her Emmeline?"

Mr. Tucker threw back his head and laughed.

"We might, my dear—but I don't think *he* would thank you for it when he got older."

Susan froze. "He?" she asked.

"Why, yes, it's a fine hearty boy! We shall call him Robert, after my father."

Susan looked so surprised that everyone laughed. Mama said something to Mr. Custer, and the two of them stood talking for a moment in soft voices about someone who had "had a hard time of it"—but what "it" was Charlotte couldn't tell. It didn't matter, for nothing Mr. Custer had to say could top the important news that now Susan had a baby too.

Susan's face looked as if she couldn't

decide whether to be happy or sad.

"Don't worry," Charlotte told her. "Brothers are nice too."

"I know." Susan sighed. "But I did want to have a sister so I could call her Emmeline."

Charlotte nodded sympathetically. Robert was a nice-enough name, but it was nothing compared to Emmeline.

Then she jumped, and her hand went to her apron pocket. "Suppose—" she said, taking out the clothespin doll and cradling her tenderly, "suppose we called *her* Emmeline! But only if you want to," she added.

Susan did want to. "It's perfect," she said, and Charlotte agreed.

Pounded Cheese

September came, and the school term was over. One afternoon Charlotte went into the kitchen and found Mama furiously pounding a cheese with a mortar and pestle. With each stroke she thumped the pestle against the mortar so hard, the table shook beneath it. Mama's eyes snapped with anger, and there were bright-red spots on her cheeks.

Charlotte could see that she was angry about something Lydia was reading from a newspaper. Lydia sat at the end of the table, holding Mary on her lap and pushing Mary's hands away from the words as she read.

Lydia's voice was impatient and bored. She did not like reading aloud. She looked up eagerly when Mama threw down her pestle and said, "I've heard enough, Lydia. Your father will be wantin' to hear this when he comes in, and I dinna think I can stomach it twice."

Lydia sighed with relief. Charlotte came to stand at the edge of the table. Mama scraped the creamy softened cheese out of the mortar into a redware mixing bowl. Her spoon made a clattering sound against the mortar, which was a large hollowed-out circle of stone, like a shallow bowl. Mama took another chunk of cheese that had been cut from one of the big round cheeses in the cellar and put it into the mortar.

Using the rounded knob on the end of the stone pestle, she pushed and ground on the hard cheese to soften it. She put a little butter in with the cheese, to make it creamier.

"Charlotte, fetch a cloth to cover that bowl.

The flies will be all over it," Mama said. Her voice was still sharp and angry. Charlotte hurried to cover the bowl of pounded cheese. Flies walked upon the floury surface of the table, and they walked in crowds on the ceiling. They lit upon the cloth that covered the dish of butter. They tried to light on the cheese in the mortar, but Mama swiped them away.

"How dare they!" she fumed. Charlotte thought she meant the flies, but then Mama said, "I can well see why me own grandfathers died tryin' to come out from under the thumb of the English. Settin' fire to our own capital city! 'Tis barbaric!" She pounded the cheese so hard, Charlotte thought the mortar would crack in two. Lydia, catching Charlotte's eye, made a little worried grimace.

"Boston's on fire?" Charlotte asked, horrified. All those houses she had seen from the Neck—and the copper dome of the State House gleaming in the sunlight—suppose they had burned down! And if they had—perhaps the British would come to Roxbury next. She had not known a war could bring such terrible things.

But Mama looked up from her pounding, and her angry gaze softened. "Och, nay, darlin', not Boston. 'Tis Washington City they've burned, those scoundrels. The capital of the United States! Their navy sailed right up the Potomac and landed an army. Set fire to the President's house, they did!" She was still angry, her lips thin and white, but it was a kind of bold, defiant anger that made Charlotte feel somehow safe. Nothing bad could happen in Roxbury, as long as Mama and Papa were here. And Boston had not burned down. That shining copper roof was still there safe on its hill.

"Mama!" Lewis came running into the kitchen, his hair sticking up wildly on his head. "Have you heard? The British—"

Mama cut him off, nodding grimly. "Aye. I went to Bacon's for coffee—not that there was anything decent, thanks to that cursed blockade—such low-quality stuff I've never seen in all me life." *Thump, thump* went the pestle in the mortar. "But the place was packed to the gills with folks talkin' about the attack. The minister was there, and they got him to stand up and read a letter from Ebenezer Craft's brother in Baltimore. Fights in the Maryland militia, he does. His unit was driven back by the British at Bladensburg." As she spoke, she scraped the rest of the pounded cheese into the redware bowl and set the mortar and pestle aside.

Lewis's eyes shone with excitement. "I wish I'd been there—I'd have given them what for!"

"Lewis Tucker!" Mama cried. "Bite your tongue, lad! I thank heaven you're too young for any militia to take you."

Lewis, avoiding her eye, gave a heavy sigh. Mama turned toward the mantel shelf to take down the spices for the cheese, and Lewis took the opportunity to relieve his feelings by making a face at Lydia behind Mama's back. Lydia opened her mouth to tattle, then thought better of it and snapped her mouth shut.

Mama brought jars of pepper and curry to the table. Charlotte watched as she sprinkled the spices generously into the creamy cheese-and-butter mixture. The smell of the curry powder made Charlotte's mouth water. Pounded cheese was one of her favorite dishes. Mama had learned the recipe from a neighbor lady last year; it was exotic and rich, and since spices were so expensive because of the war, it was not a dish Mama made very often. Charlotte couldn't wait for tea. That cheese would taste delicious, spread on slices of bread tonight.

"Papa sent me over to tell you he'll not be home until late tonight," Lewis said. "He says you aren't to hold tea for him. Half the neighborhood has come in wanting some iron-work done today."

"More than half, I'd say," said a voice in the open doorway. It was Mrs. Waitt, the miller's wife; she stood on the threshold clutching a news sheet in her hand. Perched on her head was a very large bonnet made of dark, braided straw and adorned with a lot of rust-red ribbon. The ribbon was tied in a huge nodding bow in the front, and three black feathers stuck up at the back of the bonnet, making it look a great deal like a large, well-fed chicken sitting on its nest.

"Good day, Martha," Mrs. Waitt called out. "Lydia, Charlotte, Lewis." She stepped forward and chucked Mary under her chin. "I see you've heard the news," she said to Mama, rattling the newspaper.

"Aye," said Mama grimly, reaching for another spice jar. "I was at Bacon's this morning."

Mrs. Waitt nodded knowingly. She was a small woman, rail thin, and when she bobbed her head, Charlotte thought the bonnet looked more than ever like a fat hen perched on a fence post. "I'm surprised you had to go that far," Mrs. Waitt said. "Young Lewis is right—such a crowd in front of the smithy as you never saw."

Mama snorted. "And how's Lew supposed to get anything done wi' all those men standin' about, I'd like to know? Ironwork, my eye. What they want is a place to stand

around jawin' about the attack, that's what."
She shook black pepper into the bowl, and
the cayenne that was red as her own hair. It
made a dust cloud above the mixing bowl.
"They'll be there past dark, drainin' our cider
barrels and shoutin' about how if only *they'd*
been in Washington City last week, Mrs.
Madison wouldna have had to watch her
house burn down."

She fixed Lewis with a fierce glare, for he
had all but said the same thing. He ducked
his head and nodded sheepishly. But then his
face grew sober and he said, "I don't care if
I *am* too young to join the militia, Mama. If
the British come here, I'll fight them anyway,
before I'd let them set fire to our house."

Mama's eyes grew gentle. "Aye, lad, I know
you would. But it'll not come to that. They
may try for Baltimore, but they'll never get
it. And there's no reason in the world for
the British to attack Boston—not with half
our merchants doin' trade wi' them on the
sly, and makin' a tidy profit off it, too, the
rogues." The fierce note had come back into

her voice. "I'm no supporter of this war either, but I'd never go behind me own country's back to sell to the enemy. That's treason, it is, and it's a terrible wrong."

Lewis nodded. He seemed to Charlotte to have grown suddenly very much older. He stood nearly as tall as Mama, and he was taller than Mrs. Waitt (though not as tall as her bonnet). Charlotte felt a little awed by him. He knew as much about the war as a grown-up.

Lewis must have felt her staring at him, for he looked her way. He winked at her. Then, bowing to Mrs. Waitt, he said he must get back to the shop.

"Tell your father I'll send his supper out to the smithy," Mama said. "I'll not have me husband starvin' to death just because the British have no decency."

Lewis nodded and hurried out the door. Mama pulled out a chair for Mrs. Waitt and told Lydia to put the baby on the floor. "Charlotte, you see that she stays well away from the fire."

"Yes, Mama," said Charlotte. She pulled

Mary into the corner, among the pumpkins and the squash. She built a box with pumpkins for walls and put Mary inside it, and made her laugh by making the small round acorn squash hop up onto the pumpkins like little speckled frogs.

Mama told Lydia to slice up some bread. The fire crackled busily, and the wind carried the scent of pine needles into the kitchen. It was all very cheerful except for the endless talk of the war—for Mama and Mrs. Waitt went on discussing the attack on Washington until Charlotte thought she knew as much about it as Lewis did.

The British had mowed down the American troops at Bladensburg, a little town not far from Washington City. By the time the English army reached the capital, they had defeated all the American forces in the area— much to Mama's disgust.

"They say 'twas no more than fifteen minutes' work for them to take the city," she said to Mrs. Waitt. "Mrs. Madison was just sittin' down to dinner when she heard that

Admiral—what's his name, Cockburn—was practically on her doorstep."

"Yes, I heard that too," said Mrs. Waitt. "But they say she was cool as a cucumber. She even had the presence of mind to save General Washington's portrait, God bless her. She's a great woman, is Dolley Madison."

The clock chimed five in the parlor. Mama jumped. "I'd no idea it was so late," she said. "Will you stay for tea, Sarah?"

"Oh, I'm afraid I must run home," said Mrs. Waitt, shaking her head ruefully. "I'd love to stay, but I left Henry watching the soup, and I never know but that I'll come home to find the broth boiled clean away and my best kettle ruined. You don't know how fortunate you are, having so many daughters, Martha."

Mama smiled.

"Lydia," she said, "run out and call Tom and Lewis away from the shop. They can eat here wi' us, and I'll send Lewis down afterward wi' supper for your father and Will."

Lydia ran outside, and Mrs. Waitt left just

behind her. Soon Lydia and the boys came clattering in, and it was time to wash hands and faces and set the table. Since Papa wasn't there, Mama asked Lewis to say grace. Then she passed around the platter of slices of bread spread thickly with the creamy, spicy pounded cheese.

Charlotte took a big bite. She had chewed and swallowed it before the burning began— a spicy fire that made her gasp and brought tears to her eyes. It didn't taste like any pounded cheese she'd had before. Lydia clapped a hand to her mouth, and Lewis let out a muffled shout. He grabbed his mug of cider and gulped it down. Tom was chewing slowly, a funny strained look on his face.

Mama had been spooning cold porridge into Mary's mouth, but now she stopped and looked around the table in surprise.

"What in heaven?" she said, staring perplexed at Tom's watering eyes and at Lewis fanning his mouth with his hand. "Lewis Tucker, where be your manners!"

"Beg pardon," Lewis blurted. He took

another drink of his cider. Charlotte, following his example, drained her mug. It felt cool and wonderful on her stinging tongue.

"Whatever is the matter wi' you children?" Mama asked.

Charlotte and Tom exchanged a glance. Mama was in such a state about the attack, no one wanted to make it worse.

"Well?" demanded Mama.

"The cheese, Mama," Lewis muttered. "It's a little . . ." He trailed off.

"What about it?" Mama asked, but Lewis only shrugged apologetically.

"I think . . . I think there's too much cayenne, Mama," said Lydia.

"What? Nonsense."

Charlotte remembered how the red powder had made a dust cloud over the bowl while Mama talked to Mrs. Waitt. Lydia was right. But Charlotte was not going to be the one to tell Mama that.

"It's not so bad, Mama," said Lewis. "Just caught me by surprise, that's all."

"That's right, Mama," said Tom, and he

bravely took another big bite. But it made him cough and gasp until Mama had to pour him another mugful of cider.

"Good Lord, how bad can it be?" said Mama, and she tasted a little of the cheese. Her face turned red.

"Great lairds of thunder!" she cried. "This is terrible! We canna eat this! It wouldna be fit for a pig, if we had one!"

She stood abruptly, her chair scraping against the floor behind her. "Pass me your plates, everyone. I'll not have me poor family burnin' their tongues off to spare me feelings. It's those blast— those confounded British. I was that distracted about the attack, I didna know whether I was comin' or goin', making supper."

Quickly around the table she went, scraping the bread and cheese onto a plate. "It's bread and butter for us tonight, my dears. And not much bread, at that. There's half a loaf left, but we must save some for your father. I suppose I can open a jar of pickles. But first—" She looked around the table with a gleam in her eye. "Follow me."

All the rest of her life Charlotte would remember the half hour that followed. Mama led them all out to the garden, back to a far corner where mint had escaped its tidy patch, spreading in a fragrant tangle along the stone wall. Night was falling; orange beams slanted toward the earth beneath gray billows of cloud.

"Fetch a spade, Lewis," Mama said, and Lewis ran to the lean-to while Mama cleared a space on the ground by pulling up the mint in great handfuls. The air was drowned in the smell of mint.

Charlotte and Lydia and Tom stood in a half ring around Mama, Mary wriggling on Lydia's hip. A light wind laughed in the tops of the maple trees, then raced off to wrap itself in the smoke of a hearth fire. An owl screeched somewhere over the sheep pasture. Charlotte knew from the sound that it was the barn owl that lived above the haymow; Will had pointed it out to her last summer, a funny little hunched shape sleeping in the rafters.

The rattling leaves and the cool, sharp air whispered of autumn, and Charlotte realized suddenly that she was cold in her thin summer dress. But nothing in the world could have made her go inside just then.

Lewis came back with the spade. Mama took it and, kneeling, dug a hole in the earth. The good musty smell of soil mingled with the mint and the woodsmoke.

"What are you going to do, Mama?" Tom asked. Laughing, Mama murmured, "From dust ye come and to dust ye shall return." She scraped the pounded cheese into the hole. Charlotte gasped, for though she had guessed what Mama meant to do, it still surprised her. Food must never be wasted, *never.* The cheese had been ruined past eating, but Charlotte knew that some mothers would have made their children force it down, just to keep it from going to waste.

Mama heaped dirt over the pale mess in the hole, and then she said, "Pack it well in. I'll not have cheese sourin' in my garden after the next rain."

For a moment none of them moved. Charlotte looked at Lydia and Lydia looked at Charlotte. Tom stared wide-eyed at Mama, and it was Lewis who finally stepped onto the mound of soil and began to stomp his legs up and down.

"Is that the best you can do?" teased Mama, and she stepped forward and began to dance a little jig on top of the buried cheese.

"Give us a tune, Lydia," she said.

"Sing?" Lydia asked.

"Aye, unless you've a fiddle in your pocket!"

So Lydia sang her favorite song, about a farmer and his dog.

> "*A farmer he had a pretty little dog,*
> *Called his name 'Old Bingo,'*
> *B-I-N-G-O,*
> *Called his name 'Old Bingo'!*"

Lewis held out his hands to Charlotte. She grabbed them, and he danced her round and round, singing along with Lydia in his loud, exuberant voice. Tom took Mama's hands, and Lydia whirled in circles with Mary in her arms.

> *"B with an I, I with an N, N with a G,*
> *G with an O,*
> *B-I-N-G-O,*
> *Called his name 'Old Bingo'!"*

The scent of crushed mint was thick as a cloak. Their voices rang out in the quiet air; it was as if even the birds had hushed to listen to them. Charlotte wondered if Papa could hear them down in the smithy. Perhaps if they sang louder, even the British would hear them in far-off Washington City and would know not to come near, not to so much as set a foot in the direction of Roxbury.

The sun slipped below the feathery line of the trees beyond Mr. Heath's back pasture. Night had fallen, but Mama went on dancing, so the rest of them did too.

In the Smithy

Sometimes, during the bright cold afternoons of fall, Charlotte ran across the road to the smithy, to watch Papa and Will at work. Its whitewashed walls gleamed like snow against the scarlet and golden leaves of the trees that bordered Mr. Heath's back pasture. Gray smoke swirled up from the chimney, and the roar of the forge was louder than the wind.

When she crept into the shop, Charlotte felt shy, for there were always so many people inside. Papa's customers liked to stay and talk, trading stories and news.

Often there were three or four of Tom's friends as well, playing in the open doorway and pretending to be blacksmiths themselves. They envied Tom, for he had chores to do inside the shop. Tom pushed his broom around importantly and made a show of straightening the tools upon the shelf, whether they needed it or not.

Charlotte didn't see what was so impressive about sweeping and tidying up. She did it at home every day of the year, and no one ever came to watch *her* at work.

But she understood why the boys liked to watch Papa and Will. It was exciting to see them use their hammers and pincers to twist and shape the hot iron as if it were taffy. The muscles stood out on Papa's arms, and drops of sweat ran down his face. When he wiped his forehead with the back of an arm, he left black streaks above his eyebrows.

What Charlotte liked best of all was watching Papa put on a set of horseshoes. The horses were like people, every one different;

but Papa knew them all. He spoke to them in Gaelic, the language he had grown up with in Scotland, and it was as if it were a secret language known only by Papa and horses. Their ears pricked up and followed Papa as he went from leg to leg, lifting each one gently and cradling it on his leather apron while he looked for cracks in the hooves.

Sometimes a horse was brought in because it had lost a shoe in the fields. Other times it was just that a few months had passed since the last shoeing; the hooves had grown, and the shoes were no longer a perfect fit. Then Papa used his pincers to pull the out the nails that held the shoes to the hooves. He went all around the horse, lifting the strong legs and pulling off the shoes.

Next he wiped away any dried mud and gravel that stuck to the sole of the foot. He used his knife to pare each hoof down, taking off the dead parts. Hooves, Charlotte knew, were like fingernails. Every so often they must be trimmed.

Now he was ready to put the shoes back on.

Sometimes there was wear left in the old shoes, and Papa could reuse those. But if the old shoes were worn too thin, he flung them onto the horseshoe pile. The pile was a mountain of shoes against one wall. It was taller than Charlotte, taller even than Lydia. Charlotte liked to watch that horseshoe pile grow taller week after week. Lewis told her that when the pile reached the eaves, Papa would sell all the old shoes to a traveling scrap man.

When Papa made new horseshoes, he started with a long, thin bar of pig iron. Resting the iron on the hot coals, he nodded to Lewis. Lewis pulled the long handle of the bellows to send air hissing onto the coals, making them burn hotter.

The coals glowed white as moons. When the black iron turned red, it was melted enough to be cut. With his great pincers, Papa snipped off a piece just the right size for a shoe. He made it look as easy as cutting butter with a knife.

He put the rest of the pig iron aside and began to shape the short piece into a shoe. Again he laid it on the coals, and when it glowed red, he used his long-handled tongs to remove it. He struck the iron with a hammer, slowly bending it to the right shape. Every time the hammer crashed down, sparks flew off the iron, shining in the air like lightning bugs.

In and out of the coals the iron went, until at last it looked like a proper horseshoe. He made all four shoes, one after another. Next he had to fit them to the horse's feet, and so once more he laid a shoe on the coals until it glowed red.

Sometimes the horse sidestepped nervously as Papa came near with the glowing shoe. Its ears pricked back and forth. But Papa went calmly to its side and slid his free hand along the rump and down a hind leg. He pulled the leg up and rested it on his leather apron, between his knees.

Quickly he touched the hot iron to the hoof. It hissed and sent up a cloud of smoke. Charlotte knew the horse couldn't feel anything, and it only bobbed its head out of skittishness.

"Tha sin math," Papa murmured. "Easy, now." He took the shoe away and thrust it into the water barrel beside him. Steam hissed off the water. When Papa pulled the shoe out, it was no longer red.

Again Papa cradled the heavy foot on his apron. He put the shoe against the hoof and held out his hand. Lewis was right there, with a handful of horseshoe nails ready and waiting. One by one Papa hammered the nails into the hoof. Then he took out his knife again, to trim the hoof around the shoe and make sure the shoe fit properly. He put the foot down and let the horse step on it, testing it out.

Then he began again with the second shoe.

Will could do all those things too. But Papa did it most often, because he liked the horses so much. While Papa worked, Will would be busy at other things. All day long customers streamed in and out of the smithy, bringing in tools to be repaired, or asking for a new set of andirons for the fireplace, or a spider-legged pot to set over the coals of a kitchen hearth.

Will liked to talk as he worked, and his strong voice carried over the roar of the fire and the clang of his hammer on the hot iron. He kept up a running conversation with the men who leaned against the walls discussing the war, or the price of sugar, or Chester Hutchinson's three-legged pig.

While they talked, Lewis hurried about, keeping the water barrel full, putting more coal on the fire, and fetching tools for Papa and Will. And all the time, he was hanging on every word the men said. He made Charlotte think of the horses pricking their ears and following Papa's every move.

One day a man came in waving a news-paper. It seemed to Charlotte that she met newspapers at every turn these days. She could not remember seeing them so often before.

"The British attacked Baltimore!" the man

shouted. There was an uproar in the shop, with all the men talking at once. Lewis stood frozen with his broom in his hand.

"Baltimore!" he cried.

"That's right," the man said. His name was Mr. Davis; Charlotte knew him from church. "They came down hard on Fort McHenry. But we held 'em off."

Charlotte wasn't sure where Baltimore was, but it seemed to be near Washington City, which Charlotte knew wan't too close. She must not be frightened. Anyhow, Mama had said the British would not come to Boston.

Mr. Davis said there was an uncommonly fine account of the battle in the paper.

"Seems this lawyer fella, Mr. Key, was sent out to one of the British ships," he said, "to get 'em to release one of our men, a doctor. Key did his job all right, but by the time them British agreed to release the man, the bombing had started, and it was too late for Key and the doctor to get back to shore. They had to stay there on that ship all night, watching our fort get blasted by the British navy, including the very ship they were standing on. Key told the papers it was the most harrowing night of his life. Said it got too dark after a while for him to make sense of what was happening, and for all he could tell, Fort McHenry was a pile of rubble."

"Heaven to Pete," murmured Will.

"You said it," agreed Mr. Davis. "Key said he like to cried the next morning, when the sun came up and he saw our flag still flying over the fort. Then he knew we'd won the battle and everything would be all right."

"I wish I'd been there!" Lewis said longingly.

"Well, young man, this Mr. Key—seem's he's something of a poet, too. He went home and wrote some verses about what happened. You hear them, feels like you *are* there, standing right beside him on the deck of that ship." He held up the newspaper again. "Every paper in the country is printing it this week. It's called 'Defense of Fort McHenry.'"

"Let's hear it, Davis," said one of the other men.

Mr. Davis nodded, and he unfolded the news sheet and read:

"Oh! say, can you see, by the dawn's early
light,
What so proudly we hailed at the twilight's
last gleaming?
Whose broad stripes and bright stars,
through the perilous fight,
O'er the ramparts we watched were so
gallantly streaming?
And the rockets' red glare, the bombs
bursting in air,
Gave proof through the night that our flag
was still there.
Oh! say, does that star-spangled banner yet
wave
O'er the land of the free and the home of the
brave?

"On the shore, dimly seen through the mist of
the deep,
Where the foe's haughty host in dread silence
reposes,

What is that which the breeze, o'er the
towering steep,
As it fitfully blows, half conceals, half
discloses?
Now it catches the gleam of the morning's
first beam,
In full glory reflected, now shines on the
stream.
'Tis the star-spangled banner. Oh! long may
it wave
O'er the land of the free and the home of the
brave!

Mr. Davis was right. Charlotte did not understand all of it, but the rockets, the bombs—she could see them flashing in the sky like the fireworks that rained over the common on Independence Day. And she saw the flag with its fifteen white stars glowing over Fort McHenry. Lewis stood stock-still with his mouth open and his eyes shining. Papa wiped his eyes.

"Ah, that's grand," he said.

"Yes, it is," said Mr. Davis. "This Francis

Key is a fine poet. My hired man says folks have set it to music already—you know that old air 'Anacreon in Heaven'? That's the tune. Fits these verses like it was made for them."

Papa nodded. He knew the song. That evening he brought home a copy of the newspaper and asked Mama to sing the verses.

The parlor fire crackled and the wind beat on the windowpanes. Charlotte and Lydia sat with clasped hands, and the boys stopped in the middle of their game of jackstraws to listen. Mary was asleep in Papa's lap, her little mouth pushed into an O against his shoulder.

Will sat near the fire with his chair tipped back, staring at the flames, his brown eyes serious and shadowed.

The candle burning on the table beside Mama's chair cast a yellow glow across her and made her red hair glow like fire. Her voice rang out like a bell.

> *"Oh! thus be it ever when freemen shall stand*
> *Between their loved home and the war's*
> *desolation,*

In the Smithy

Blest with vict'ry and peace, may the
  Heav'n-rescued land
Praise the Pow'r that hath made and
  preserved us a nation.
Then conquer we must, when our cause it is
  just,
And this be our motto, 'In God is our trust.'
And the star-spangled banner in triumph
  shall wave
O'er the land of the free and the home of the
  brave."

Apple Time

In October four of Papa's customers paid him in apples. Mama sent a great many of them to Mr. Heath, to be made into cider in his cider press; she kept a basket of russets in the kitchen for the children to eat.

Charlotte ran outdoors in the crisp autumn air with apples and Emmeline bouncing in her apron pockets. She felt sorry for Emmeline, who nearly always wound up squished under apples at the bottom of the pocket, but it could not be helped: the apples were that delicious.

Tom ate a dozen green apples on a dare and got so sick he spent three days in bed. After that he wouldn't eat apples for a month, not even when Mama served apple pie with dinner. Mama shrugged and said he could go hungry if he liked, for that left more pie for the rest of them. But Tom ate twice as much chicken stew as everyone else, so he didn't go hungry at all.

Even after apple pie and cider and all the apples eaten out in the yard or munched at night before the fire, there were bushels of apples left. These must be peeled and cored and sliced, and hung to dry. Charlotte thought that was the very best thing about apples, for it meant apple-paring parties.

All the neighbors held them, and Mama held one too. First she and Lydia and Charlotte had to clean the house from top to bottom; Charlotte hated that part, but it could not be blamed on the party. Autumn housecleaning must be done, apples or not.

The cleaning took a whole week. After it was done, Mama sent word to the ladies of

the neighborhood that she was having a
paring the next evening after tea. Charlotte
and Lydia were allowed to walk across the
long fields to Mrs. Heath's house to invite
her. Will had an errand on Centre Street, and
Mama asked him to stop at the tin shop and
leave word for Susan's mother. Charlotte
could hardly sleep that night, wondering if
Susan would come. She had barely seen her
since school had ended, except for a few minutes before and after church.

Susan did come. Her mother brought the
baby, too, well wrapped in bunting, and all
the other ladies gathered around to admire
him. Mrs. Heath chucked him under the chin
and asked Miss Heath if he didn't have the
wisest eyes she'd ever seen on a baby. Miss
Heath agreed and begged Mrs. Custer for a
chance to hold him.

"Goodness, such a little dear!" she said,
kissing his cheeks.

Susan rolled her eyes at Charlotte. "I
don't see why everyone makes such a fuss,"
she whispered. "He doesn't *do* anything,

except sleep and eat and cry."

"At least he doesn't try to eat your doll," Charlotte said. But they only pretended not to like their babies. Really they liked them very much.

The parlor was so full of people—and apples—there was hardly room to move. The hearth fire glowed, and candles made the room bright. At first the noise of greetings and taking off of coats and wraps was so big, it seemed bigger than the house. But quickly all the ladies settled into chairs and took up the knives they'd brought from home. The confusion of noise subsided to a loud, laughing murmur of gossip and news.

Charlotte and Susan sat squeezed together on a little bench Mama had asked Lewis to bring down from the boys' room. They talked and talked, and there was so much to talk about, it seemed as though there could not be enough apples in all the world to keep their mothers busy long enough. They watched the ladies move quickly through the baskets of apples, peeling and coring and slicing them.

Lydia and some other big girls had been given needles and string, and they strung the apple slices on long strands that Papa and Will hung from the rafters. The apples would hang there in merry festoons until they were well dried out. This was how Mama made the apples last through the year, for dried apples kept far longer than fresh ones.

Miss Heath and some of the other young ladies played a game with their apple peels. They cut the peel off in one long spiraling piece, and when they were done, they closed their eyes and threw the peels over their shoulders. Then they looked to see if the peels had fallen to the floor in the shape of a letter. Miss Heath's peel looked like an S, and that meant she would marry a man whose first name started with S. Miss Heath blushed when she saw it and made a face that was meant to look angry but wasn't really, the same way Charlotte and Susan had pretended not to like their babies.

Miss Hannah Stowe, the cooper's oldest daughter, said teasingly, "Oh, what a pity Sam

Dudley isn't here; I hear tell he threw an apple peel and it spelled 'A'!" Then Miss Heath blushed all the more and tried to hide how pleased she was.

Charlotte thought it was a very silly game. Apple snap was much more fun; she begged Mama to let the children play it, and Mama said they might. Will tied a whole apple to a string and hung it from the ceiling. Each child had a turn at trying to take a bite out of the apple without using hands. The apple swung back and forth; Charlotte's teeth snapped on the air every time.

Tom was the best at getting bites. He got the most bites, but Lydia got the biggest. Mary stood beneath the apple with her arms outstretched, crying, "Me, me, me!" until Lewis picked her up for a try. She was too little to understand the game; she grabbed at the apple with her chubby hands and pulled it right off the string. She looked so pleased with herself that no one could be angry with her, and Mama said it went to show that sometimes the smallest could be mightiest.

It was a lovely, laughing evening, and when it was over, Charlotte thought nothing could be half as much fun, ever again. But then the Heaths held a paring in their big white farmhouse, and that time Charlotte won the apple snap. So that party was even better than Mama's had been.

There had not been much news of the war since the attack on Baltimore. Papa went to a meeting at the town hall one afternoon, and when he came home, Lewis would not give him a moment's peace until Papa said that yes, the vote had passed, Roxbury's militia was going to stand in defense of the country. A unit would go up north to fight the British near the Canadian border. Lewis jumped up and down at the news, and Will listened silently with a strange light in his eyes. Mama did not toss her head and scoff, as she had so often done when the war was being talked about; she had a look on her face that was very like Will's. Charlotte watched the grownups talk and wondered why it was that they cared so much about things that seemed very unimportant to her, and yet they did not take notice of the really important things.

Most important was the Saturday night when the molasses father came back to the table. For two whole days Mama had boiled cider in the big iron kettle until it became thick and syrupy, and she said it was cider molasses. It didn't taste quite the same as real cane molasses. But Charlotte was so glad to see the jolly father jug back in his place on the table that she wouldn't have cared if it tasted like water. This was the Saturday family's last chance to be all together again for a long time, for the cows had stopped giving milk and there would be no more butter for the butter baby until spring.

With the molasses jug back where it belonged, Charlotte could almost forget there was a war going on at all. But that night, after supper, Papa said something to Mama that brought the war rushing back into the house like a gust of cold wind.

He came into the kitchen and pulled a chair up to the fire while Mama washed the dishes. Charlotte and Lydia hurried back and forth from the parlor, clearing the table.

Papa said, "Will's unit musters on Monday noon. Suppose we pack a picnic lunch and go to see him off?"

Charlotte stood frozen before the kitchen cupboard with the molasses father in one hand and the vinegar mother in the other.

"Aye," Mama said, sliding a plate into the tin washpan, "and I'll fill a basket for the lad as well. Has a long march ahead of him, he does."

She gave a little sigh, and Papa nodded. Charlotte stared at them, but they did not notice her.

Lydia came in from the parlor with her hands full of dishes. "What are you doing?" she asked Charlotte. "A snail would move faster."

Charlotte hardly dared to ask; she was afraid of the answer. "Is Will leaving?" she whispered.

Lydia looked at her in surprise. "Why of course he is! He's joined the militia! Didn't you know?" And then she cried, "Oh, Charlotte!"

For Charlotte had dropped the Saturday father. The little redware jug had slipped from her hand and crashed to the floor. It lay in pieces, and the molasses made a sticky pool on the sand.

Charlotte stared at it, horrorstruck. Tears sprang to her eyes and she cried out a word that was supposed to be "No!" but did not sound like a word at all.

"What on earth?" Mama said, turning toward the cupboard with her dishcloth in hand. Papa half stood up from his chair.

Charlotte could not move. Lydia took the vinegar cruet from her hand, saying, "Here, you don't want to drop that too," and all at once Charlotte was sobbing and running.

She ran through the lean-to and out to the barn. Patience and Mollie looked up from their stalls with their mouths full of hay. Their brown eyes glistened in the dim light. The sheep made soft bleating noises from their pen.

Charlotte climbed up the ladder into the hay-mow. She threw herself down on the blanket of hay. The sweet golden smell of hay was so strong, she could almost taste it through her tears.

One of the barn cats came and nosed around Charlotte's head, but Charlotte did not look up. Stupid cat, to think it could help.

She heard steps upon the barn floor, and then upon the rungs of the ladder, and she knew it was probably Lewis, sent to find her. Well, he could just go back inside. But a hand touched her hair, and it was not Lewis's hand. In spite of herself Charlotte raised her head to look. It was Mama, kneeling beside her in the hay with her skirts tucked up like a little girl. She didn't say a word, just sat Charlotte up and held her close as she smoothed the damp curls off her face.

For a long time there was just the low grunting sound of the cows chewing their bites of hay. Then Mama said, looking around at the mounded hay and the lacy cobwebs in the rafters, "Would you believe I've never once been up here in all the years we've lived here?"

"Truly?" Charlotte said, in spite of herself. It was surprising to think of—that Mama had lived here so long, and yet here was a place Charlotte came to before Mama did.

"Truly. 'Tis rather nice, is it not?"

Charlotte gave the tiniest, tiniest nod. She did not feel like agreeing that anything was nice, just now. She picked up a piece of straw and broke it into small, sharp bits.

"Mama," she said, "is Will really going away?"

"Aye, that he is. I'm that proud of him, too. 'Tis a brave thing and a noble one, to fight for your country, Charlotte."

"But—" Charlotte groped for words, but all she could say was "I don't want him to leave."

"Whisht, we mustn't think of ourselves just now, lass. I'll miss him, too, him wi' his rogue's smile and the manners of a king. And your papa will have a hard time findin' someone so clever and hardworkin' as Will to help him in the shop." Mama sighed. Her hands moved absently, picking bits of straw out of Charlotte's hair. "But Will feels he must go, and I must say I agree wi' him. I'd rather we'd stayed out of this war altogether, but we're in it now, and the army needs good brave lads like Will to kick those British soldiers back to England."

"Why are the British here, Mama? Why won't they leave us alone?"

"Well, as far as that goes," Mama said, "'tis America that declared war on England, not the other way round. Some people believe—President Madison is one of them—that America had no choice but to stand up to England and tell her she'd better think twice about tryin' to bully us—stealin' our sailors, sellin' guns to the Indians, and such like. We're a new country, you see, and we've got to show the world we're strong enough to look after ourselves. *That's* why we're at war, Charlotte. That's why Will is going to fight."

"Will he come back?" Charlotte asked. Her voice was very small.

Mama sighed again. "We must pray that he

will, Lottie, and leave the rest to God. That is all I can tell you."

Charlotte balled up her fists in the hay and cried, "I hate this war! I hate it!" She knew it was naughty to speak that way, but she didn't care.

"Hush, now," Mama said. "There's a great many folks feel that way, but you dinna hear them wailin' about it. Here you are in a fine snug house, safe and sound, wi' plenty o' food on the table. There's folks in Boston feelin' a much tighter pinch than we are, wi' their trade cut in half by the blockade. Not to mention all the poor souls down in Bladensburg, or up on the Niagara, who've had their homes burned out over their heads by British troops. We're that lucky, Charlotte Tucker, we ought to be on our knees every day thankin' God for what we've got."

But Charlotte did not feel the least bit thankful. She thought of the molasses, a dark pool spreading over the white sand on the floor.

"I broke the molasses jug," she said miserably.

"I know," Mama said. "We shall have to go to Bacon's and pick us out a new one."

"But it won't be the same!"

Mama shook her head gently. "Nay, lass, it willna be the same."

Charlotte leaned against Mama and cried as though she were a baby of Mary's age. The Saturday father was gone; she had killed him, *killed* him. Will was going away. It didn't matter that the British would not come to Boston; Will was going to them. Nothing would be the same, not ever.

The Seagull

On Monday morning Will came home—
only it was not his home, not anymore. He carried a lumpy burlap sack
and an old musket that his father had used in
the War for Independence, many years ago.

There was no fire in the smithy's forge that
day. It was a strange kind of morning that
was not a workday and not a Sunday. Mama
bustled about the kitchen packing a picnic
lunch, and a separate bundle of food for Will
in a checkered napkin. Will protested, saying
his mother had already given him food

185

enough for the whole army, but Mama ignored him, with a look in her eye that said wild horses couldn't stop her from sending Will off with some of her ginger cookies.

"Perhaps you should make me some pounded cheese, Mrs. Tucker," said Will, grinning wickedly. Of course he knew all about the cayenne disaster; Mama had told him and Papa herself. "If I could sneak it into the enemy's rations, they'd cry all the way back to England!"

"Whisht!" Mama said, tossing her head. "Give a lad a musket and he turns saucy on you!"

Charlotte did not see how anyone could make jokes today. She was not sure she wanted to go to the common to see Will off. But Mama said of course she must come; everyone must.

"You should bring Emmeline, too—she'll not want to miss hearing the drums," Mama said, so Charlotte tucked Emmeline into her apron pocket and stood quietly while Mama tied on her bonnet.

Lewis led the way past the smithy and the mill, toward the white spire of the meeting-house and the wide square of Roxbury Common. There was a great crowd in the common. Men in top hats stood importantly on the steps of the new town hall, looking out upon the soldiers in their untidy rows on the grass.

People milled in and out among the soldiers, saying good-bye. Mothers hugged lanky young men, who rolled their eyes with embarrassment but whose Adam's apples moved up and down in a swallowing, home-sick kind of way. Fathers clapped their sons on the back, and sweethearts held each other by the fingertips.

To her delight, Charlotte spotted Susan in the crowd. She waved, and Susan turned and said something to her mother. Mrs. Custer nodded her head, and Susan ran to join the Tuckers. Charlotte was so glad to see her that she let Susan carry Emmeline for a while. The doll's bright face looked calmly upon the mass of people, as if such crowds were nothing new to her.

Will craned his neck around, searching for someone, and then his face lit up and he said, "Ah, there they are. Come, I want you all to meet my family."

He pushed through the crowd to a wagon standing on the roadside near the meeting-house. A tall man with a wide-brimmed hat stood beside the horses; seated on the wagon box were two ladies in plain knitted shawls and straw bonnets. Will introduced them to Mama and Papa. The tall man was his father, and the older of the ladies was his mother. She had his same smiling eyes, and just now they gleamed with a proud light.

The younger lady was Will's Lucy. Charlotte forgot that staring was impolite, and she stared so hard that Lydia had to nudge her before she remembered to curtsy. Then she blushed and curtsied hastily.

Lucy was not nearly as pretty as Miss Heath. She had a crooked mouth and a pale face that was marked with smallpox scars. But her smile was warm and lively, and her eyes were piercing blue. She leaned forward and gave Mama her hand.

"I'm so pleased to meet you, Mrs. Tucker," she said. "I've heard so much about all of you."

"And we of ye, as my mother's old cook used to say." Mama grinned. "I'm in the way of understandin' that we're to be neighbors when Will returns to us."

Lucy smiled again, this time at Will. "Yes, and I'm counting the days," she said frankly. Will smiled back. His mother said, "Really, Lucy!" and clucked her tongue a little.

But Mama laughed and said, "I should think you would be!"

Lucy invited Charlotte and Susan to sit on the wagon seat with her for a spell. Papa lifted them up, and they looked out upon a sea of hats and bonnets. Charlotte had not known there were so many people in Roxbury. Lewis and Tom ran about with some other boys, playing soldiers. After a while Mama said Lydia must have a turn on the wagon. Will helped Charlotte and Susan climb down.

"Look," called Lewis. "There's the captain. What's he shouting?"

"He's calling us to form ranks," Will said. Suddenly everyone was crowding around him to say good-bye. Charlotte hung back, but Will came to her and gave her shoulders a squeeze.

"I'll keep my eyes out for corbies when we march up north," he said. "You never know but one of them might take it into his head to have a look at the New World!"

Charlotte shook her head. "No, Will. You know they only live in Scotland."

"Ah, but the world is changing all the time, Charlotte," Will said, his voice gentle and low. "Just because something has always been one way, that doesn't mean it will go on being that way forever."

Charlotte knew he was talking about more than just corbies. He watched her, waiting, but Charlotte didn't know what to say.

It was time for him to go. Taking up his two food bundles—the one from his mother and the one from Mama—he touched his hat and said, "Well, I'm off!" and strode away toward the lines of soldiers in the center of the common.

Mama wiped a tear from her eye, which surprised Charlotte. Mama never cried. The ache in Charlotte's throat was worse than crying. She looked for Will among the other soldiers but could not see him. The men looked all alike with their newly oiled muskets slung over their shoulders and their proud, determined faces staring straight ahead.

The captain, a stout man in a soldier's uniform, held up his sword. All the soldiers stood at attention in their rows. The rows were ragged and uneven, for this was only a militia unit, not the regular army. The captain made a speech, and then the mayor of Roxbury made one.

Then the captain gave another signal, and the drummer began to play. Next to him a soldier raised a fife to his lips. A shrill birdlike piping soared above the crowd. It was the tune of "Yankee Doodle," and its notes rang out clear and pure above the crowd. The soldiers began to march. They marched out of the grassy square and filed down Washington Street.

Past the town hall, past the grand houses along the square, past Mr. Bacon's store they went, and the crowd of townspeople went behind them.

"Come, let's follow!" Susan cried, tugging Charlotte's hand. So they ran with the other children, following close behind the proudly marching soldiers.

When they reached the Neck, the crowd of children came to a stop. Charlotte stood on the side of the road, watching the soldiers march away toward Boston. The tide was in, making a bridge of the road. On both sides of the marching soldiers the water stretched out broad and blue. Sunlight sparkled on the water and dazzled Charlotte's eyes. All around her the little waves glinted like the glint of the sun on the copper dome of the State House, across the bay at the edge of the sky.

All this time Susan had been holding Emmeline. But now she slipped the doll back into Charlotte's hand. Charlotte squeezed Emmeline, hard. She didn't know how hard she was squeezing until Susan giggled and said, "Lucky thing she's made from a clothespin and not a corn husk."

That made Charlotte laugh. She looked at Susan, and all at once she felt better. The war was taking Will away, and it had broken up the Saturday family. But if it hadn't been for the war, Susan would not have come to Roxbury. To think Charlotte might have sat alone on the bench all summer at school! And Emmeline would not be named Emmeline— perhaps she would still be nameless, the poor thing.

Charlotte could never choose between Will and Susan. She wouldn't want to. She began to see what Mama had meant about leaving things to God.

A seagull squawked from a fence post beside her. It might have been the same fence post and the same seagull Charlotte had seen before, the day she tried to walk to Boston. The bird had a gray head and wings the color of old snow. It stared at Charlotte with a round black eye. If Will were here, he could tell her what kind of seagull it was, and where it had started out, and where it was going. But the soldiers were halfway across the Neck now, growing smaller step by step.

The gull spread its pointed wings and soared into the air. Charlotte watched it sail high over the heads of the soldiers and out above the glittering water.

Keep your eye on Will, Charlotte wanted to tell it. *Can you see him, I wonder?* That made her think of the words of Mr. Key's song: "Oh! say, can you see . . . ?" Of course the gull could see, for it could fly so high that it was higher than Great Hill. It could watch over Will in the crowd of soldiers; it could see the whole of Boston. It could see the British frigates and sloops-of-war blocking the harbor, and Susan's father's ships waiting at the docks for the war to be won. It could go anywhere, see everything, and Charlotte wished with all her heart that she could go with it and see what *it* saw, out there in the wide world beyond Washington Street.

Come Home to
Little House

The LAURA *Years*
By Laura Ingalls Wilder
Illustrated by Garth Williams

The CAROLINE *Years*
By Maria D. Wilkes
Illustrated by Dan Andreasen

The MARTHA *Years*
By Melissa Wiley
Illustrated by Renée Graef

The ROSE *Years*
By Roger Lea MacBride
Illustrated by Dan Andreasen
& David Gilleece